Books By Lily Thomas

Giant Wars Series
Loving His Fire
Grounded By Love
Melted By Love
Wicked Flames of Desire

Galactic Courtship Series
Xacier's Prize
Claiming His Champion
Captivating the Doctor
Escaping the Hunt
Abducting the Ambassador
Wicked Prisoner
Seducing the Enemy
Cuff Me Now
Challenging the Arena
Dark Desires in Space
His Fallen Star
His Human Temptation
Racing Toward Desire
Zro'eq's Fallen Star
His Human Doctor
The Spy and The Alien
Her Desert Alien

Ice Age Alphas
The Sabertooth's Promise

The Sabertooth's Mate
Direwolf's Desire

Her Desert Alien

Lily S. Thomas

Chapter 1

Knock. Knock.

Hazel rolled over in bed, enjoying the feel of her soft sheets against her skin. "Go away!" She buried her face in her pillow, willing the pleasant dream back into existence. It'd been about a man. A man who could only be created by a dream. Perfect smile. Perfect teeth. Perfect hair. Tall and muscular.

Where was her dream?

She grumbled into the pillow with impatience as she waited for her dream to reappear. She wanted her mister dreamy back.

Knock. Knock.

"Go away!" What part of her sentence did they not understand? Hazel rolled over again. She fluffed her pillow a bit with her hands as she settled back down, and when what seemed like a few minutes passed without any interruption, she relaxed a bit.

Knock! Knock! Knock!

"Fine!" Hazel bellowed at the person banging on her door. As her brain woke and the fog cleared, she heard a commotion outside. Voices yelled, and she could make out a few harsh words.

Popping up in bed suddenly, Hazel shook the sleep from her head and glanced around. It was early morning, just after the sun rose… barely. The weak beams of sunlight shot through her open window where she'd allowed the night air to cool her bedroom off.

With a growl, Hazel swung her legs out of bed and trudged over to the bedroom door. Everyone in their colony knew not to wake her this early. She was the grumpiest morning person ever.

"What?!" She barked as she yanked the door open, nearly popping her shoulder out of place.

"Hazel…" Her father's eyes dropped as his mouth opened in shock, and then he slammed his hands across his eyes. "You're naked!"

What?

Hazel glanced dumbly at her father, who cowered behind his hands and the men behind him who gawked with a mixture of horror and fascination at her nudity.

"For Pete's sake, woman, close the damn door!" Her father cried when he peeked between a couple of fingers and saw her still standing with the door wide open.

"You brought me to a desert planet where it's boiling during the day and hot at night." Hazel pursed her lips as she cocked a hip, completely unfazed about her nudity. She wasn't ashamed of her body, and she firmly believed nudity wasn't something to be embarrassed by. "I sleep naked."

"Get dressed, Hazel. Our crops are on fire, and we need all hands on deck." Her father reached out with a hand while turning his head and grabbed a hold of the door handle before shutting it with a wham.

A fire!

Their crops!

Hazel didn't waste a single second. Sprinting over to her closet, she slid the metal door back on its rollers and grabbed the first things she could get her hands on. There was no need to look nice or care about what she wore when their crops were on fire. Maybe if her father had led with that, she would have jumped into action.

Once she finished dancing around her room as she tugged the clothing into place and pulled her golden hair into a messy bun, she bolted for her bedroom door.

Hazel sprinted through the hallways, which were made of broken-down spaceships from when her people had traveled here and established a colony. Her boots thundered over the metal floors, and her heart pounded as she wondered how bad the fire was in the crop field.

As she burst through the hatch and landed on the sand outside, she froze in her tracks. The glow of red and orange lit up the grey early morning sky, and a billow of smoke rose high into the air. This wasn't a small fire.

Getting her sudden panic under control, Hazel darted for the nearest set of staircases and quickly climbed them to the curtain wall they'd built around their small colony to keep out the beasts that roamed the desert planet at night.

Once to the top, Hazel got her first glimpse of the devastation below. All that work. All of the hard work with the relentless sun beating down on their heads and backs as they painstakingly farmed their crops… it was all gone!

Hazel's hand gripped the metal of the curtain wall as she watched men scurrying around below, trying to get the blaze under control and salvage as many plants as they could.

It didn't look promising.

Hearing male voices somewhere nearby, Hazel turned her gaze from the fire and spotted her father standing among some men just a bit further down the wall. She walked over to them, a pit forming in her stomach when she noticed their grim expressions.

Sidling up to the men, she listened in to the conversation.

"It was those aliens," Emmanuel said to her father, his green eyes flashed with a spark of fire as he looked to the other men to back his statement.

"We should bring the fight to them." Layton backed Emmanuel eagerly as he rubbed his hands in front of him.

Hazel frowned as she listened to the conversation. One bad deed did not deserve another. There had to be a way for their colony to co-exist with the aliens. They couldn't leave. Their colony had deconstructed their space ships when they landed on the desert planet, and only then had they discovered their mistake.

The desert planet was already occupied.

Here her father thought he'd found the perfect planet, free of complications for their colony of humans who wanted to break free of Earth and the aliens who complicated everything.

Hazel hadn't minded living in space with the excitement of never knowing what could happen. Still, she'd been reluctant to abandon her father when she found out he was serious about starting up a colony.

Her father snorted, "How do you plan on

bringing the fight to them, Emmanuel? We don't even know how to reach them. They live underground, and we don't know where the entrance is."

"We can find it." Emmanuel looked around at the men as he nodded his head.

"I didn't start this colony to see our people go to war. I started this colony to take us away from Earth's wars and problems. To seek a place where we could find peace and quiet and live out our lives." Her father frowned at all of them. "We don't know why the aliens attacked, and we need to figure it out."

"I think they made it clear," Layton growled between clenched teeth. "They don't want us here and are willing to destroy our crops… to destroy us. This," Layton waved an arm at the burning fields, "is our food source. We only have enough seed for one more try, and if they burn that?"

"We won't give them a chance." Dougie finally entered the conversation, his deep baritone carrying easily through the noise of the crackling fire and yelling of men as they attempted to get the fire under control. "We can post guards at night to make sure the aliens don't get another chance."

It sounded reasonable to Hazel. Posting some guards would prevent the aliens from destroying another crop cycle, and it would keep them from war… she hoped. Oh, she really hoped. She hadn't wanted to come to this planet in the first place, but her father was her only family, and she'd felt obligated to join him lest she lost contact with him.

Emmanuel looked to her father, a frown on his lips as he crossed his arms over his chest. "You are the leader of our colony, what should we do, Erik."

Her father took a second, and she saw his blue eyes churning as he thought over their discussion. "We will try Dougie's idea. We will post guards within shouting distance all around the crop field… and we will give them weapons, in case the aliens come armed. It isn't a long-term solution, but it will have to do for now."

The other three men nodded before heading off to oversee her father's orders and to assist with the fire.

"Dad?" Hazel smiled at her father as she took a couple of steps forward.

"Hazel." Her father smiled warmly at her. "Sorry to wake you so early, dear, but all of us are out here, and it's only fair you help with the fire."

Hazel held up a hand. "Say no more. I understand I need to be here to help." She turned to leave and then paused, "Do you think this will escalate further than crops?"

She heard her father heave a sigh from behind her. "Only time will tell. I'm sorry I brought you here, Hazel."

Hazel spun around. "Even with the current events, I would still choose to be by your side." She sprinted forward and wrapped her father in a bear hug. "We will figure this out together, and I agree with what you decided."

Her father's arms wrapped around her, giving her a light squeeze before placing a kiss to the top of her head. "Ever since your mom left us, I've done my best to raise you and keep you safe, and I feel as though I may have failed this time."

"No, you haven't." Hazel shook her head

against his strong chest. "You did what you thought was better for us, and I'm an adult who chose to follow you, like all the other colonists here. We believe in you."

"You always know how to cheer me up." Her father chuckled before releasing her. "Now go and help before anyone accuses me of favoritism."

"I'll go!" Hazel sprinted back over to the stairs and climbed down. Time to head out to the crop fields.

Chapter 2

The heat from the leaping flames seared Hazel's face with warmth, and as the sun rose over their desert planet, sweat pooled between her shoulder blades and on her forehead. It was like basking in a sauna, and she could go with a glass of water, but they had to ration water, especially now that they were using up so much water on putting out this fire.

Theo ran up to her and dropped his metal bucket at her feet with a hollow clank. Hazel handed him a full one with water a bit sloshing over the sides.

"Thanks, Hazel." Theo sent her a warm smile.

Hazel gave him a nod in return, hesitant to provide him with a smile lest she got him thinking that she returned his feelings. Theo was charming and perfect. For another girl. He was handsome with strong chiseled features, and a dimpled chin. His sun-bleached hair and grey eyes would snag him many women if their small colony had more women his age and single.

"You're welcome," Hazel mumbled before bending over and grabbing the discarded metal pale and handing it off to another woman standing nearby.

A woman on Hazel's other side passed her another full bucket, and Hazel waited for the next man to sprint over and handed it off.

The fire was almost out, but it had managed to chew through most of their field. Gone were the crops. They would have to start all over, which meant they would have to ration their food even more while they waited for the second batch of crops to produce.

Ugh.

Grey blob-like rations. They didn't taste better than fresh food.

"I was thinking we could meet up at some point." Theo ran back over, dropped his bucket on the ground, and grabbed the full bucket out of Hazel's hands. "A date?"

"Ummm, is now the time to ask?" Hazel didn't think fighting a fire and asking for dates went together. Although, if she were any other woman, she might be flattered that he thought her attractive while sweat-soaked. Instead, she wished he would turn his attentions elsewhere in the colony.

"No better time." Theo's smile grew larger before sprinting back over to the flames.

Ugh.

No!

Hazel had hoped to avoid this. She never wanted it to come up.

She handed off another full bucket of water to another man.

Theo always took the time to send her a smile and talk with her. She knew this moment would come when he would ask her out, but he wasn't her type. There was no way she could imagine being with him for the rest of her life… or having children.

Oh goodness.

Children involved sex.

She couldn't have sex with Theo. She preferred the tall, dark, and handsome men. Blonde men didn't do it for her, and then there was his personality. Every time she stared into his grey eyes, she swore she could see something dark lingering back there.

"Seems Theo is sweet on you."

Hazel glanced over to see Maggie standing beside her with a bucket full of water. Her usually puffing black hair was flat against her head with all the sweat her body produced to cool her down. "This fire is horrible." She tried to change the subject.

"It is." Maggie shook her head, sending her wet black curls waving around her heart-shaped face. "But, it did get Theo to finally ask you out." She rolled her eyes. "We've all been waiting for him to get the courage."

Hazel grimaced as she passed off another full bucket. She'd really hoped Theo never got the courage. "How should I turn him down?"

"What?" Maggie's head nearly turned off her head as she whipped around and gazed wide-eyed at Hazel. "Why would you want to do that? He's the most attractive man under thirty in this colony." Maggie grimaced. "Sometimes, I wish I never came. I hadn't thought about there not being enough attractive men to go around."

Hazel handed off yet another bucket of water. "Neither had I."

As much as she hated to agree with Maggie, Theo was the most attractive here, and she could do worse. He was a kind man as well as easy on the eyes, but there was still something lingering in that soul of his.

"The fire is out!"

The cry of excitement had Hazel's head shooting up where she saw that the men had indeed gotten the last flames of the fire put out. A relieved smile turned the corners of her mouth as she walked back to the well with her bucket of water, pulled off the metal lid of the well, and poured the water back in.

Maggie walked over and did the same with her bucket of water. "Thank goodness we put it out."

"Yeah." Hazel turned and surveyed the field. "Sadly, I don't think much if anything survived the fire." Most of the crops had been burnt to ash and those that hadn't were just blackened sticks standing up out of the soil.

"We will have to replant." Maggie agreed with a sigh. "If you thought the first time was hard, this time will be even worse, because now we will need it to work before we run out of food."

Hazel sucked in a shaky breath. Perhaps they shouldn't have deconstructed all of their ships. Now they were stuck here on this desert planet with no way off. They could try sending a signal into space, but they would have to wait for a passing space ship to hear it, and then they would have to hope they weren't space pirates.

An image of sand burying her sun-scorched bones had her quivering in fear. Or one of the many carnivorous reptiles that roamed the surface of the planet would lick her bones of flesh after she perished of starvation.

But that wouldn't happen!

Hazel sucked in some calming breathes through her nose and let them out of her mouth.

Everyone here wanted to survive, and she had to believe they would find a way to survive.

A couple of days later, Hazel stood on the curtain wall, looking out at the desert mountains on the west side of the colony. The mountains were just as dry as the rest of the planet. The gnarled trees were long dead, just brown stumps withering away slowly through time. The mountains were riddled with ginormous caverns and canyons.

A roar went up in the distance. It was faint, but her ears picked up on it. Surveying the land around them, she tried to spot the source of the sound, but it was either too far away to see, or it was hidden behind a sand dune in the distance.

The desert lizards were enormous, nearly the same size as a small two-person shuttle, and they would love a human snack.

Turning her attention away from the desert, Hazel glanced down at the crop field. From here on the wall, she had the best view of the burned crops. A few crops had survived, but they wouldn't be enough to feed the colony. They would still have to replant and try again.

"Hazel!"

Hazel's head swiveled around while her body continued to face forward. "Maggie?"

Maggie bounded up the metal stairs, taking the stairs two at a time until she reached the top and swiftly walked over to Hazel. "I thought you might like to know that a meeting was called to discuss the aliens again."

"I thought we made a decision on how to handle them burning the crops." Hazel's eyebrows drew down over her eyes as confusion rolled through her. She was pretty sure the conversation between her father and the other men had been real and not a dream.

"It seems the men posted around the crop field have seen more evidence of aliens," Maggie shrugged, "but all of this is second-hand information, so take it with a grain of salt."

"Where are they meeting?"

"In the cafeteria." Maggie raised a hand and pointed a finger towards the other building like Hazel had no idea where it was located.

"Thanks." Hazel sprinted over to the stairs and pounded her way down the steps.

"Wait for me!" Maggie called out, but Hazel wasn't about to waste time waiting around.

If only they had known aliens lived on this planet before settling down. Unfortunately, when they had scanned the surface of the planet, they found it lifeless except for the few alien creatures that lived on the surface, but they didn't think about scanning under the surface. If they had, they would have found the planet was already populated.

When Hazel reached the double metal doors of the cafeteria, she paused for a second before straightening her blue t-shirt and smoothing any loose blonde strands behind her ears. Then she reached out and pulled back on the handle.

Walking into the cafeteria, she found a fair amount of the colony within the small room. The chairs were arranged to face a raised platform where her father and the other advisors of the colony sat.

"What are they saying?" Maggie whispered beside her as Hazel closed the door silently behind her.

"I don't know. I just got here." Hazel whispered back before finding a seat at the back of the room.

Maggie plopped down on the empty seat next to her as they both listened with interest.

"We need to do something about the aliens." Someone seated in the crowd tossed out.

Her father nodded his head. "We have guards posted around the crop fields."

"We should do something more." Another person complained. "They feel free to attack us."

Maggie hissed under her breath, "They seem to forget we started this."

Hazel glanced over at her friend. "You mean when some of the young men encountered that alien a few months ago?" Hazel had forgotten about that.

"Yeah," Maggie whispered behind a raised hand as she leaned in towards Hazel. "Didn't you hear what happened?"

"No." Hazel shook her head. "What happened?" And how had she missed this piece of gossip? In a colony where the daily chores were the same, and meals were pre-scheduled, any piece of excitement was hard to miss.

"As I heard it, our men killed the alien with a plasma pistol."

Hazel sucked in a harsh breath. "So, the attacks on us and our crops were provoked." She hadn't known that. She knew about the skirmish, but somehow, she'd never learned about the death of the alien. No wonder they were being attacked!

"I mean," Maggie held up a hand, "I'm not defending the aliens and their actions, but we did start it."

Hazel nodded her head as she turned her attention back to the discussion.

"Maybe we should bring the fight to them." A young man stood up, and Hazel didn't miss the arm that reached up and dragged him back down to his seat. Probably the young man's mother.

She rolled her eyes. The aliens lived underground, giving them a tactical advantage. Starting a war would be stupid. Really stupid. From what she heard, the aliens were impressive in size and possessed the same kind of technology. However, she couldn't confirm anything since she had yet to set eyes on any of these aliens. All she knew about them was from other people, and when people were scared, they tended to get details wrong, like saying something was bigger and scarier than it really was.

"We should bring the fight to them." Another person latched onto the young man's declaration. "They clearly want to wipe us out, maybe we should take them out first."

Hazel shoved herself to her feet. "I think that would be a mistake."

All the people in front of her shifted in their seats and turned their eyes on her. A lump formed in Hazel's throat as she stared at all the faces. Some lips were drawn back in displeasure at her outburst, and some looked on encouragingly.

Maggie reached out and slid her hand into Hazel's and gave it a comforting squeeze.

Clearing her throat, Hazel slowly looked around the room and met everyone's gaze. "I know we started this colony to separate ourselves from aliens, and Earth, and the complications of space, but do we really want to start complications here, with these aliens?" She met some of the colonists' eyes. "We can work out something with the aliens. I am sure they want to live their lives in peace just like us."

"And how would we go about talking with them?" Emmanuel asked her from where he sat up on the platform with her father.

"I'm sure we can find a way." Hazel shrugged. She wasn't entirely sure how to let the aliens know they wanted peace, but there had to be a way. "We can send someone out to meet with them or leave them a message on a tree. We can find a way."

Her father raised a hand to his mouth and coughed as he stood. "You'll have to excuse my daughter. I don't think she understands the gravity of this situation."

"Clearly not." Emmanuel scoffed, earning himself a glare from both Hazel and her father.

"Why can't we send an envoy?" Hazel placed her hands on her hips. How dare her father act like her idea was childish or insane. Her suggestion of peace was not crazy!

"She means well," her father continued, "but we are too far for negotiations, and we can't risk sending an envoy lest the aliens send their heads back to us."

With the wind taken out of her sails, Hazel plopped down on her seat.

"Hey," Maggie wrapped an arm around her shoulders, "you tried."

"He just dismissed me," Hazel waved her hand toward her father, "like my opinion didn't matter." Hazel felt her heart hitch in her chest. "He's never dismissed me before."

"It's a tense situation." Maggie's hazel eyes swirled with sympathy. "He may just be uttering things he'll regret later. It's a lot of pressure being the leader of a colony with no one else to call on for help. He has to make sure he makes the right decisions."

Hazel heaved a sigh. "You're probably right." Her father's words still hurt. She'd left her space-age life to join him on a desert planet, so they wouldn't lose contact, and now she wasn't even sure he appreciated what she left to be with him. A job, a potential love interest, and she'd given her pet away.

Maggie patted her hand.

The rest of the meeting passed in a blur of raised voices as the crowd got riled up, and it seemed the consensus was that they should bring the fight to the aliens before the aliens brought it to them. It disappointed Hazel. They were only causing drama here on their little planet. Their little planet that was supposed to be a haven from the dramas of Earth.

As the cafeteria emptied of people, Hazel followed them in a daze until a hand reached out of nowhere and roughly pulled her out of the crowd of moving bodies. When she glanced up, she found her father's face glowering down at her.

"Yes?" She asked a bit tartly, still pissed that he'd shut her down earlier in front of everyone in the colony.

"I want to encourage you to speak your mind, Hazel, but you need to learn to read a crowd."

Hazel's mouth fell into a flat line as she glared at her father. This man who shared genes with her was turning out not to be the man she thought he was. He should want to pursue peace rather than pick up arms against the aliens.

"Not everyone wants to go to war with the aliens, dad." Hazel folded her arms in front of her chest. "We came here to escape these kinds of complications."

"We did, but we also need to defend ourselves." He clamped a hand back on her shoulder as he met her eyes. "I would offer up a peaceful resolution to the aliens, but I can't send anyone out there. No one would volunteer either, because I can't promise they won't be killed."

Seeing she wouldn't get anywhere with her father and not wanting to be a part of this fight anymore, Hazel said, "I don't know what I was thinking. You're right. I should have read the crowd better."

She wasn't giving up. Just biding her time. She had to rethink her approach to her father and the people of the colony. They could still achieve peace. She would never give up on it. Never.

Her father nodded his head. A smile cracked over his lips. "We can talk more about this later if you want, and don't forget Hazel, I love you." He raised a hand and placed it against her cheek.

She leaned into his comforting touch. "I love you too, dad."

"I have things to attend, but at dinner, we will discuss this more. In the privacy of our home."

"I'll see you then." Hazel spun on a heel and left before she said something she would regret, like calling him an ass for not listening to her or taking what she said seriously. There had to be a solution. A way to reach out to the aliens.

What she needed was to find a place to relax, like the indoor gardens their colony had thanks to a botanist who traveled with them.

Hazel walked across the courtyard, kicking up dust as her booted feet shuffled across the sand. When she reached a glass door, she pressed on the metal bar and stepped inside a humid garden. It almost felt like a rainforest, and it instantly felt good on her dry skin. The dry air of the desert irritated her skin, not to mention her poor scalp.

Finding a bench, Hazel sat down and enjoyed all the leafy green plants around her. At least the fruit plants were doing well since they were safe inside the compound, unlike the crop fields. They may keep getting their crops burned, but at least they had fruit. It wouldn't be enough to survive on, but it would be better than nothing.

Her head fell back as she closed her eyes and let her skin soak up as much water as it could. She would remain here for as long as she could because it was an excellent place to find some peace and quiet. Not many people visited the gardens, which always confused her. She loved the gardens.

Within minutes, Hazel fell asleep on the bench, tired from the excitement of the day.

Chapter 3

Hazel walked across the courtyard towards the cafeteria. Each family had a designated dinner time to keep the cafeteria from being overly crowded. Their little colony only had so much room, since they used their deconstructed ships to build their colony.

After her quick nap in the garden, Hazel had gone about her daily duties, which included tending to some animals that were being raised as a source of food and helping to clean out all the ash from their crop field.

Then she'd gone back to her room and took a sonic shower. It was a shower that used blue light rather than water, so they didn't have to waste water on washing when they needed it for their plants, animals, and drinking.

As Hazel entered the cafeteria, there wasn't a single scent of food. Her face fell. It must be ration time. Darn the aliens for burning the crops. Until now, they'd always been given a hot fresh meal for dinner. With their crops growing green and strong under the desert sun, no one had feared a food shortage. Now, though, now people worried there wouldn't be enough to go around.

She walked up into a line, and within seconds she walked away with a platter full of boring grey ration. It was essentially tasteless, but it had everything a human body needed to survive.

Hazel picked a table away from other colonists. She felt a bit self-conscious since her outburst earlier in the day, and she could have sworn she felt eyes watching her. It was going to take her a bit to forgive her father for shutting her down.

"Hey, Hazel."

Glancing up, Hazel spotted Theo on the other side of her table. "Hi, Theo." She sent him a smile.

"Mind if I sit here?" He motioned to the table while holding his tray of food with his other hand.

"Yeah, sure." Hazel motioned to the spot across from her with her fork. As much as she wanted to say it was taken, she'd made the mistake of picking an empty table. Next time, she would know better.

"Thanks." Theo plopped down on the metal seat with a sigh. "I've been on my feet almost all day dealing with the crop field and tending the animals."

"Same here," Hazel said, and then they fell into an uncomfortable silence, or maybe it was just awkward for her because she felt like she had to say something but didn't know what to say.

Especially after his declaration the other day.

One side of her mouth curved in distaste, but she quickly wiped it from her face before Theo saw it.

Did this count as a date?

Hazel's eyes narrowed on Theo in front of her as she ate some of the grey blob on her tray. She wouldn't count this as a date, but she had no idea what he thought. It was lunch, and they were eating together. Then again, she was probably overthinking all of this.

Maybe there was some lucky woman she could foist him off on.

Hazel studied the cafeteria while she tried to find someone she thought Theo might like more than herself. She came up empty. Most women had come either with a husband, boyfriend, or fiancé. No wonder he was interested in her. With very little pickings, he might want to tie down a woman before she chose someone else.

Unfortunately, for Theo and everyone else here, she'd already checked out the pickings and decided there were no men who interested her. Maybe she would simply go single for the rest of her life.

"I'm going to start interning under Dr. Turner tomorrow," Theo said suddenly. "I was supposed to start today, but they really needed extra hands in the field."

"Sorry, it got pushed off. Are you excited?" Hazel really wished Theo hadn't sat down with her. This small conversation was difficult and annoying.

"Yeah. I was studying to be a doctor before I heard of this colony, and I thought it would be a great opportunity to find a place that needed my services." Theo smiled, showing off his straight white teeth. "I'll finish studying under Dr. Turner."

Wow.

Theo really was the perfect package, and she felt weird that she didn't want the package. A blonde, blue-eyed doctor in a medium-sized colony like theirs made him a catch.

If she wanted to end this attraction he had for her, then she would have to do it sooner rather than later. Leading him on would only hurt him and cause him to be angry with her.

And she couldn't date willy nilly, because if

they broke up having an ex in this small of a colony could be awkward. They would definitely bump into each other, so she had to be sure about a man before dating.

Thankfully, their dinner went by quickly and with silence, until...

"I wondered if you would like to take a stroll with me, maybe to the gardens?" Theo asked as he pushed his tray away from him, finished with his meal.

"Ummm," Hazel looked around as her brain worked double-time to think of an excuse why she wouldn't be able to join him.

"It's just a stroll." Theo pressed. "Join me." He stood suddenly and presented her with an outstretched palm.

"What are you two up to?"

Hazel grimaced as she realized it was her father. Turning slightly on her seat, she faced him. "Theo–"

"We're taking a stroll in the gardens," Theo announced proudly with a charming smile sent in her father's direction.

"Well," her father glanced over at her with a twinkle in his blue eyes, "isn't that something."

"It's something, alright." Hazel agreed with a grump as she rose from her seat.

Theo strode off toward the entrance of the cafeteria and waited by the door for her. His grey eyes filled with expectation and a smile on his lips.

"You two will make a great match." Her father winked at her. "He's going to be a doctor."

"He told me." Hazel nodded her head, less impressed than her father.

She hadn't realized joining her father in his colony meant she'd feel like a teenager again. There wasn't much room in the colony, meaning she shared living quarters with her father, which took away her freedom and another reason she shouldn't date. Bringing home men would be awkward.

"It's a good pick."

"It's a stroll, dad." Hazel shook her head as she rubbed a couple of fingers on her brow. "It's not like I'm agreeing to marriage."

"There aren't many people your age here. Either the men are too young or too old or already taken. You might want to take this a bit more seriously, Hazel." His eyes took on a steely note.

"I am," Hazel said before she marched off to join Theo.

As they entered the gardens, Hazel realized exactly why Theo had chosen the gardens. The humid environment was dense with green vegetation, and it provided a fantastic place for a romantic tryst between lovers. Too bad for him, they weren't.

They strode around the pathway in silence, and when an orange circular blossom caught her attention, Hazel bent over to smell the flower. It was sweet and delicate, and she could imagine it making a great perfume.

"I know," Theo said, breaking the silence, "that you might not want my attentions, but I'm hoping to sway your mind."

Hazel righted herself and turned, "I'm not sure…" Her words faded when Theo suddenly stepped forward, eating up the distance between them and pressed his body into hers.

"Let me sway your mind." Theo bent his head, and his lips captured her stunned lips.

Hazel's mind couldn't process what was happening. She stared dumbly at the shock of blonde hair in her field of vision. His kiss wasn't repulsive. It was nice. His lips were soft, and he smelled spicy, but it didn't feel… right. There was no spark, and she felt no need to continue the kiss.

Raising her hands to his chest, Hazel pushed him away with a sharp movement.

Theo's blue eyes widened in surprise when he realized she hadn't been under his spell, like he thought. Clearly, he'd been able to use his good looks and kissing to persuade women to give him more.

"I need more time. I don't want this to move too fast." She motioned between them. "Let's take this slow and see where it goes." It wasn't exactly a promise of dating, but it also wasn't a denial, and she knew she was threading the needle on this one.

Theo straightened his shirt as he cracked his neck side to side. "You're right. We have all our lives. We should move slowly." He held out his hand, "Let me guide you around the gardens before you head off for bed."

"Suuure."

After a few minutes of walking around the garden and chit-chatting about nothing in particular, Hazel finally broke free of Theo and made her way to her room. As she crossed the courtyard, she watched Theo out of the corner of her eye, and the moment he walked into another part of the compound, Hazel changed directions and climbed the stairs up to the metal curtain wall.

The two moons and trillions of stars were out, lighting up the desert below. It was almost romantic. If only she had a better suitor, someone who stirred her. Kissing under the moonlight while watching the stars… oh yeah. That would be the perfect date.

"I saw you and Theo leave the gardens."

Hazel gasped as she whipped around. "Maggie!"

"What were the two of you doing in there?" Maggie wiggled her eyebrows suggestively.

"Pfft," Hazel rolled her eyes, "you know nothing happened."

Maggie shook her head as she pursed one side of her mouth. "I still don't understand why you insist on pushing Theo away." She held up her hands. "I understand he isn't your type, I just find it interesting since any woman, even the married ones, sneak looks his way."

"Do you like him?" Hazel asked.

"Not my type either," Maggie laughed. "Maybe I should stop pushing you at him."

"You should!" Hazel agreed with a chuckle. "Trust me, he's doing a good job on pressing himself on me without any help."

"He," Maggie reached out and gripped Hazel's shoulder as their gazes met, "didn't press anything on you, did he?"

"What?" Hazel shook her head. "Nah, nothing like that. He kissed me in the gardens, but I shut it down pretty quickly, and he was nice about it."

"Good." Maggie smiled, relief flooding her face. "You let me know if you need help with convincing him to go somewhere else for some loving."

"I'll let you know," Hazel reassured her friend. "Do you want to know the disappointing part?"

"Of the kiss?"

Hazel nodded.

"Yeah." Maggie leaned in closer as she rested her forearms on the curtain wall, which still held some warmth from the hot day.

"When Theo kissed me, I hoped there would be sparks, but there wasn't a single one." Hazel glanced out at the desert sand dunes that surrounded them. "Is that silly of me?"

"Doesn't sound silly to me."

A dark movement in the sky had Hazel squinting her eyes, but when she tried to spot it again, she couldn't find it. It must have been her imagination or a trick of the eyes in the dark. Human vision wasn't the best at night.

"I would have pegged him as a better kisser, one that could elicit sparks."

"Whatever." Hazel shrugged. "I've agreed to date him, I guess, for now, until I figure out how to let him down easy."

"Well, I came up here to tell you about a little get together some of the younger people are having tonight. Wasn't sure if you would want to join or not, but figured you would like to be invited either way."

"Sure, why not." Hazel tossed Maggie a smile. She wouldn't mind a little party to get her mind off Theo, and hopefully, he wouldn't even be there.

"Come on, then." Maggie reached out and grabbed a hold of Hazel's hand and tugged her along.

Down the metal stairs they went, through the courtyard, and then through an archway to a door, and then they entered another section of the compound that had yet to be used for anything. The area was jam-packed with anyone under their thirties but old enough to drink.

Some music thumped in the background at a pleasant noise level, probably to make sure they didn't disturb anyone who was already asleep.

"Let's get something to drink." Maggie pulled Hazel into the party until they reached a fold-out table that was laden down with booze.

That was something every colonist had brought with them. There was plenty of alcohol. If they ever did run out of food, at least they could drink their sorrows away before the desert killed them cruelly.

"I'll take one of those," Hazel said, pointing to a woman who held a blueish drink.

The guy behind the table acting like the unofficial bartender began to create her a drink.

"I'll take a shot of whatever is the strongest," Maggie said.

When their drinks finished, they sipped them while they walked around the party. From what Hazel could see, Theo wasn't here. Thank goodness. She wasn't sure she could face him after their lackluster kiss.

Hazel sucked in a big gulp of her drink. The alcohol should clean his kiss out of her mouth.

The night faded on. The dancing grew more boisterous, and the music turned up a bit more as people got drunk and a bit less considerate of anyone sleeping elsewhere in the compound.

Hazel's eyes searched the pulsing crowd of dancers as she attempted to find Maggie, who disappeared a while ago with a man.

"I have something to say!"

Hazel's head swiveled around, but she didn't spot the source of the yelling voice.

"Hey! Shut up!"

The crowd went quiet as the music dimmed a bit. Whoever had yelled earlier had found a microphone. Well, this should be good.

"I have something to say." The person slurred, clearly well into their cups.

"This ought to be good." Someone nearby Hazel quipped, and she couldn't help the smirk that shot across her lips. A drunken speech was always the best.

"These aliens need to be shown a lesson." The drunk man continued.

People in the crowd looked around at each other, seeming undecided on where they stood on the subject.

"Come on, people! We need to show them that we can and are willing to fight back. This is our home." The man continued, and Hazel searched for the man, but where ever he was, he wasn't anywhere near her.

"Me and my buddies are willing to go out there into the desert and hunt these aliens down."

Hazel rolled her eyes, and she was pleased when the people around her murmured in disagreement. Not everyone wanted to start a war with the aliens.

"Ugh, hey, Sammie," Hazel turned to the woman nearby, "if you see Maggie, will you please tell her I went to bed? I can't listen to this guy."

"Yeah, no problem." Sammie lifted her cup in confirmation.

"Thanks." Hazel headed off to bed. Hopefully, these people would sleep off their drink and realize going to war with the aliens would be an unwise decision. In the meantime, she needed her own rest.

Chapter 4

Yelling from outside had Hazel rolling over in her bed. She cracked an eye open as she glowered at the grey sky through her open window. As much as she liked to cool her room down with night air, she was close to giving up and using her air conditioning unit. With the window shut tight, she might finally get to sleep through the morning without the colony waking her up at the crack of dawn.

"Why can't I sleep in until my alarm goes off?!" Hazel smacked a balled-up fist against her soft pillow right before she slid out of bed. Reaching over, she turned off her alarm, which was a part of her nightstand. The holographic blue numbers blinked at her.

The voices continued to yell angrily, and Hazel knew she had to get out there and see what happened overnight to cause this morning commotion.

Leaping up from her bed, Hazel grabbed a robe resting on the back of a nearby chair. After she wrapped it around her frame and tied the sash around her waist, she busted out of her room and into the courtyard.

When she got to the center of the courtyard, she spun around in a tight circle, until she spotted a crowd up on the curtain wall.

"Damn." Hazel cussed as she realized those people faced in the same direction as the crop fields.

The aliens must have come back last night. Maybe that blur, or trick of the eye she'd spotted last night, had been an alien.

She shook her head. No. She had to keep a calm and straight mind here. There would be no panicking from her.

With determination in each step, Hazel marched up the stairs and over to the group standing around on the curtain wall. Pushing through the throng of people, she made her way to the edge of the wall.

Smoke rose in front of her like a wall of grey. The last part of their crop field smoldered, men ran around below her as they tended the scorched ground.

"Again?" Hazel whispered in horror. Sure, the skirmish a few months ago had ended in an alien being killed, but did they really need to continue the offenses? There had to be a way to get through this without bloodshed or starvation.

"It's time for us to do something, Erik."

Spinning around, Hazel found Emmanuel, her father, Dougie, and Layton gathered nearby.

"How much of this are we supposed to take? Soon, they are going to kill us."

The rest of the men nodded their heads, and she found her father rubbing his chin. It was his tell. It meant he was considering what the other men said.

She kept her mouth shut, though. She'd learned her lesson. No one ever listened to her when she opened her mouth to give an opinion. From now on, she would remain silent, so no one knew she was there listening.

"What exactly do you suggest?" Her father asked as he looked to the other men around him. "They live underground. How do we bring the fight to them?"

Emmanuel looked lost for words finally, as his mind struggled to think of something to suggest. "We should think on it."

"Maybe we should go somewhere private while we toss around ideas," Dougie suggested. "We should come up with a united plan to present to our people."

The rest of the men nodded in agreement as they headed off.

Hazel pursed her lips. She couldn't handle this anymore. Someone had to try and talk to the aliens. If talk didn't work, then they could resort to other tactics. And if no one else would speak with the aliens, then she would.

Now she just had to come up with a plan.

Was this a good plan?

Probably not.

Hazel didn't feel like she had any other choice, though. No one else wanted to do to risk their lives for peace, so she would. She hefted a duffel-like backpack onto her bed after she double-checked her bedroom door was securely locked. She didn't need her father barging in to find her packing. It would raise his suspicions before she even got anywhere.

Focusing on the supplies she had spread out before her on her mattress, she triple-checked she had everything for a night out in the desert. There were a couple bottles of water, plenty of survival food bars to keep any hunger at bay, and plenty of different types of clothing, some to keep the sunlight from reaching her skin and some for the night to keep her warm.

She couldn't think of anything else she needed.

"Oh, yeah!" Hazel snapped her fingers as she bolted away from the bed and rummaged through her room until she found the plasma pistol she took out of the armory. She might need this to keep herself safe from the desert animals. Always come prepared. She would rather have something than need something.

Walking back over to the bed, she stuffed her backpack full, making sure to place the plasma pistol on the top before zipping it closed. She wanted the gun within easy access in case she needed it.

Sucking in a deep breath, Hazel steeled her nerves. What she was about to do was beyond stupid, but if she died, at least she tried to talk with the aliens. It was better than not trying at all.

Or she would go down in colony history as an idiot.

Either way, she thought she was doing something brave and for their colony.

Threading her arms through the loops on the backpack, Hazel hefted it onto her shoulders and walked over to her bedroom door. Switching the lock back, she cracked the door open and popped her head out.

The hall was empty.

Hazel crept out into the hall and did her best to tiptoe through the metal hall with her thick soled boots. "Sorry, dad. I hope you understand one day why I'm doing what I'm doing." She whispered as she passed by his door.

It was late evening, earlier than midnight, but late enough for everyone to be in bed. Her father would be tucked away and fast asleep.

She slunk her way down some stairs. Then she crept her way around the open courtyard, sticking to the side walls to blend into the night, which was only lit by the two moons hanging in the sky.

Hazel easily found the door that would allow her out into the desert. She placed her hand on the pad but froze. She was about to step out into an alien desert with no one other than herself.

If she wanted, she could slink back to her room and pretend like this never even happened, or she could follow through with her plan and see if she couldn't talk some sense into the aliens.

Firmly, Hazel pressed her hand against the pad, and the door popped as the lock freed. Then she pushed the heavy metal door open, and she took her first few steps out of the compound. As she left, she pushed the door closed until she heard the hiss of it locking again. Now she couldn't go back. The only way from here was forward.

Hazel walked most the night with only a couple of small breaks. She wanted to make it far enough away from the compound that no one would come after her when they noticed her missing, and close enough to the mountains to hopefully draw the attention of the aliens. There were guesses as to where the aliens came in and out of their underground civilization, and most of those guesses involved the mountains to the west of the compound.

The only thing that had so far inhibited her progression was the sand. Walking on sand was a ridiculous workout for her calves and thighs. The tiny brown granules shifted under her weight and sucked her boots in a bit in greedy hunger. If and when she got back to the colony, she would have some well-toned legs.

Every once in a while, Hazel heard the calls of those lizard-like reptiles. They made a noise that sounded like a mixture of a cough, a whistle, and a growl. It was an eerie nose that sent goosebumps racing across her neck.

None of the lizard creatures had ventured close, either they didn't think she looked like a tasty snack or they hadn't noticed her presence yet. Either way, she was glad for that small blessing.

Swinging her backpack around to her front while she walked, Hazel took out one of her water bottles, raised the nub to her lips, and tilted her head back. Sadly, it was already empty, and all she got was air. All this walking had worked up her thirst, but she didn't want to use up too much of her second bottle, so she put the first bottle back and pressed on.

In a few more hours, the sun rose above the horizon and began beating down on her. Lifting her gaze to the offending ball of burning gas high in the sky, she glowered at it. Sweat poured down her back and face, causing her clothing to stick to her skin uncomfortably.

Stopping, Hazel glanced back from the direction she'd come. There was no way she could make it back to the compound now that the sun was out. Looking back at the mountains, she realized all she could do was continue and hope she didn't die of heatstroke first.

Within a couple more hours, wind-twisted leafless trees began to dot the area along with massive boulders. She was at the mountains, but the sun still pounded down on her like its only mission was to halt her progress.

Holding up a hand, Hazel gave the bird to the sun as her feet dragged across the sand in a tired shuffle. She was all out of water. The second bottle had been polished off a couple hours ago. Two bottles hadn't been enough, but her body still sweated in a big gamble. The sweat would help to cool her body but at the cost of using up her precious water.

What Hazel needed to find was some shade. Shade would help keep her cool until night came. The heat would still be stifling, but it was better than being baked alive under the harsh rays. If she survived this, she would never tan another day in her life. The sun was cruel and mean, and they would never have the same comfortable relationship.

When the tip of one of Hazel's boots met a small hill of sand, it sent her tumbling to the ground, and there she stayed. She had no energy. She couldn't even get her arms to work. They laid on the piping hot sand neck to her like a couple of limp noodles. As she laid there, the image of her sun-bleached bones gleaming in the sand ran through her mind. She would die here, and no one in the colony would know what happened.

Chapter 5

The lone figure in the desert trudged its way through the desert. The figure looked so small compared to the vast desert around them. Sand stretched as far as the eye could see, and sun weary minds were easily distracted by mirages on the horizon.

The person's steps faltered, and soon the toppled over, faceplanting in the sand.

Drakkein leaned forward in interest atop a boulder. Would the figure rise?

The visor covering his face zoomed in, but he still couldn't get a clear view of the alien. Curiosity had him wishing he could see a bit more of the figure.

Ever since his people spotted the figure approaching the mountains, he and his men had been sent to the surface to find out what it was doing over here. He felt confident there was no threat from this lone figure who could barely make it through the desert heat. But the council wouldn't be happy until he figured out why the alien walked all the way over here.

After a couple of minutes, Staavo broke the silence. "Are we going to help the alien, or leave it to die under the sun?"

Drakkein glanced over at the other man, who was covered head to toe in thick black armor. Even their faces were covered by a mask of dark glass. The suits were based off their spacesuits, but these were specifically meant to protect their people from the harmful rays of the sun. Their species couldn't tolerate the sun, but they had invented these suits in case they ever ventured up to the surface of the planet.

The only part of them that they left exposed were their dark horns. Their horns never seemed bothered by the bright light, but their delicate wings were firmly tucked into their suits.

Staavo met his gaze, but Drakkein could barely see the other man's face through the glass. "I'm bored, Drakkein. Either let's rescue it, or leave it to go hunt some of those lizards." He raised his armored hands. "Let's just do something other than sit here in the shade and watch it slowly die."

"Maybe it already died, and it is too late to save it." A voice said from behind them.

Drakkein glanced behind him to see another friend, Aknan, sitting on a boulder, a plasma rifle cradled in his hands. Then he glanced back to the figure lying on the sand. It was definitely one of those aliens from the compound on the surface. That much he knew because his people were the only other ones living on this harsh desert planet.

"We will rescue it." Drakkein decided. "Perhaps if we save it from death, we can learn more about its people and their defenses. Also, if we allow it to die, the council might not be pleased we missed an opportunity to speak with one of the aliens."

"Good idea." Staavo leaped to his feet and sprinted into the sun.

The sunlight glinted off Staavo's black armor, and despite the dark glass on his visor, Drakkein raised a hand to his eyes. The sun caused nervous twinges to form in his stomach. Just one ray of light on his exposed skin would fry him. It would take a bit to kill him, but it would crisp his skin. He knew from personal experience how terrifyingly powerful the sun was for his people.

"Are you coming or not?"

Drakkein rolled his eyes as he lowered his hand. He could never teach Staavo patience. The man jittered and bounced his way through life. Sitting still was not his forte.

Rising from his crouched position in the cool shade on his boulder, Drakkein shivered as the sunlight streaked over him when he jumped to the sandy ground beside his boulder. Thankfully, his suit kept him from burning his skin. His large boots helped him to stay above the sand with ease without sinking into the shifting grains.

Staavo reached the form lying face down in the sand first. "Think it's dead?" He called out.

"Poke it, and find out," Aknan called back.

Staavo poked the figure with a booted foot, but the figure didn't make any noise. "I think it died."

Drakkein glanced down at the figure when he pulled up beside Staavo. "Ugly thing, isn't it?"

Staavo grunted in agreement.

The long sandy hair had been darkened with streaks of sweat, plastering the strands to the alien's head. A large sweat spot soaked the back of the shirt, darkening the material and causing the clothes to fit firmly against its body.

Drakkein cocked his head to the side as he took in the alien. It was short. He had to be at least a head taller if not more, and it looked defenseless like it had been born with no physical attributes that would assist in defending itself. He almost pitied the alien lying at his feet.

"Think the aliens are usually this red?" Staavo hunched down and poked an armor covered finger against the skin. When he pulled the finger away, the skin looked white, but with the blink of an eye, it flooded back up with the angry color.

"I don't think they are supposed to look like casso fruit," Drakkein replied.

"Should we leave the body for scavengers?" Aknan asked.

"Are we sure it is dead?" Drakkein bent down and rolled it over. "It's female." Her face was just as burned as the rest of her body. Turning his wrist, he typed in a few commands on the face plate of his wrist. Then he pointed it at the body and waited.

Beep. Beep.

Drakkein glanced back down at the device. "She's alive. It's reading a heartbeat and breathing."

"Do we bring her back to the city?" Staavo asked. "I know the council wanted us to find out more, but she could also be a security threat."

"She's nearly dead." Aknan reasoned. "One alien can't be too much for us to handle. It's not like we are inviting their whole colony into our city."

"We bring her back." If Drakkein could get her to one of their medics, he had no doubt they would save her life. Then his people could learn something about these aliens who had landed on their planet. It didn't look like the aliens would be leaving anytime soon, so they needed to know more.

Placing his hands under the alien woman, he

tilted her back until she slid into his arms, and then he gathered her close to his armored chest as he stood. The woman didn't even open her eyes or make any noise. The sun didn't appear to blend well with her species either.

"Here I looked forward to some hunting, but I guess that won't happen now," Staavo complained like a despondent child.

"We'll get back out here once we drop her off, right?" Aknan asked, also sounding hopeful that they could still go hunting.

"Yes, once we get her to our hospital, we will come back out," Drakkein promised his men because he too wanted to hunt down some of the large reptiles roaming the desert. The lizards were good eating and their people's main source of meat.

As they walked over the baking sand, Drakkein breathed a sigh of relief the moment they stepped into the shadow of a sand dune. Even with the suit encasing his body, the sun caused him to sweat a bit between the shoulders. If the suit were to be ripped off, or fall off, as impossible as it sounded, the sun would sear across his skin. It was an irrational fear because as long as he wore his suit, everything would be fine, but he still remembered his mistake when he had been a child.

A shiver rolled through him as he broke out into the sunlight again.

Somehow, as a child, Drakkein slipped past his nanny and found his way to the surface with only his simple day to day clothing. To say he'd been burned would be an understatement, but the experience had given him a greater respect of the sun.

After a couple of months of being cloistered away in their hospital until his skin fully healed, he'd sworn he would never make that mistake again.

Shifting the woman in his arms, Drakkein paused when he reached the door. Anyone outside of their city would never guess it was a door. It was a camouflaged door. The outside looked rocky and brown, matching the side of the mountain.

"Can you hold your wrist up to the door?" Drakkein asked one of the other men as he sidestepped to allow them access. "I can't twist my arm that way while holding her."

"I can." Staavo stepped forward, held his wrist up to the door, and then they all heard the click as the door unlocked. Staavo stepped aside as the door swung open, revealing a dark corridor lit with green lighting.

A smile spread across Drakkein's face when the dark interior revealed its shaded cool inside. Within a few quick steps, the darkness enveloped him, and the trickle of fear that always floated in the back of his mind vanished. No sunlight would be able to reach his sensitive skin inside the thick mountain.

After they all entered the mountain corridor, the thick metal door closed behind them. Their boots rang off the purplish metal floor, echoing off the metal walls until they broke into a locker room.

Drakkein placed the alien on the floor.

Backing away, he joined the other men as they peeled off their armor. "Wait." Drakkein held out a hand. "You two stay in your armor. Once I have her dropped off with the medics, I'll come back so we can hunt."

"We'll be here," Staavo said as Drakkein peeled the last piece of his suit off and stashed it inside one of the many lockers lining the walls.

Striding back over to the alien female, he kneeled next to her, gathered her into his arms, and strode out of the locker room. When he arrived at a balcony overlooking their underground city, he glanced at the stairs and then the balcony. It would be faster for him to fly to the hospital rather than walk there.

Unfurling the leathery wings on his back, Drakkein stepped up to a gate in the rail, pushed lightly on it with a foot, until it swung wide. Drakkein tipped over and let gravity pull him over the edge. As he fell through the air, he heard the gate swing closed behind him to prevent the young and old from falling to their deaths.

Then he flung his wings wide, and they caught on the air with a small jerk before allowing him to soar through the large cavity that separated two sides of the city. He wasn't the only Aeci soaring through the city. Other people flew around as they went about their daily lives.

It only took a few minutes to navigate his way through the lights of the city, zooming above and below bridges made of both metal and rock, and spot the landing pad for the hospital.

Spreading his wings wide, Drakkein slowed his descent as he angled his feet towards the ledge. He landed with a bit of force, but he recovered quickly by walking a couple of steps. Folding his wings tightly behind his back, he strode through the sliding metal door of the hospital.

"How can I help you?" A woman rose from her seat from behind a desk, and he recognized her to be Ein, a nurse who always seemed to be on duty. Then her eyes widened as she caught sight of what Drakkein carried. "Is that…" She pointed a finger at the woman in his arms, "is that one of those aliens from the surface?" She stepped around her counter to get a better look at the woman in Drakkein's arms.

"She is, and I need you to save her life, assuming she's still alive." He glanced down at the woman in his arms, but he couldn't see from his angle if her chest moved or not.

"We can do that. Can you keep carrying her?" Ein cocked her head to the side as she absently rubbed a hand over one of the horns on her head.

Drakkein nodded his head.

"Then follow me." Ein motioned him forward. As she led him through the hallways of their hospital, her wings waved lightly with her steps.

Drakkein glanced down at the alien woman in his arms. Her sunburned skin was so distinctly different than his silvery skin, which everyone in his species had. She was a dainty thing compared to him, and she had no claws, wings, significantly sharp teeth, or any natural defenses he could see. He wondered if the males of her species had more defenses.

"Here we are." Ein waved a hand at an open door to a room. "Just set her down on the bed, and we will take care of her… as best as we can."

Drakkein glanced behind him as he stepped through the threshold. "What do you mean?"

"We don't know her species." Ein smiled kindly. "Depending on the severity of her injuries, we might not know how to help her."

"I don't think she is injured. She just had too much sun." Drakkein explained as he laid the alien woman down on the bed and backed away.

"If that's all, I don't think we will have any issues assisting her." Ein washed her hands in a sonic sink. Blue light emanated from the device, cleaning her hands before she grabbed a needle. "Are you going to stay while we tend to her?"

Drakkein shook his head. "No, but I'll be back later to check in on her."

Ein nodded her head before returning her attention back to the alien woman, and Drakkein left without another look to meet back up with Staavo and Aknan.

"Think the alien woman will make it?" Staavo asked through the radios that each of them had in their suit helmets.

"Ein seems to believe they can heal the woman," Drakkein said as he hefted his plasma rifle in his hand. They were on the surface of the planet once more, and this time, they were tracking a grakid rather than one of the aliens. It was a reptile… a very large ill-tempered reptile with sharp teeth and a jaw that could crush just about anything.

A small wind built, blowing the particles of sand all over the place and swiftly covering the large footprints they'd been following through the desert.

Staavo cursed under his breath. "We'll have to head in the same direction and hope we come across some more tracks."

"Lead the way," Drakkein said, as he surveyed the land around them. Sand stretched as far as the eye could see, and when he glanced in the opposite direction, dry mountains greeted him. Any water this planet held was deep down under the surface and hard to reach, which was another reason his people lived under the surface, where they were closer to the only source of water.

"I've found some more tracks," Staavo said, his voice transmitting through their helmets.

Drakkein walked up beside his friend and looked down at the sand where there was indeed a claw print. A huge claw print belonging to the biggest predator on this planet. Their small hunting group moved on until they rounded a sand dune and froze in place.

Right in front of them stood a giant reptile with tan and white scales covering its massive body. The beast huffed and puffed, sending sand particles flying into the air. Apparently, they weren't the only ones hunting today. The large beast seemed to be searching for prey.

"How do we want to approach it?" Staavo asked as they stood there behind the snorting reptile.

"Aknan, do you think you can circle around from the other side without attracting its attention?" Drakkein asked, while never letting his eyes stray from the beast.

"I can do my best," Aknan replied before stepping away from them and heading around the other side of the sand dune.

Staavo and Drakkein waited motionless as the reptile swooshed its long scaly tail across the sand as it continued searching the ground for something. What it searched for, Drakkein had no clue, since his sense of smell was nowhere close to this beast's sense of smell.

"I'm in position." Aknan's voice came through their helmets.

"Aim your weapons for its soft underbelly, and let's hope it goes down quickly," Drakkein said, as he quickly fingered the blade at his back. If it came down to close combat, they always carried at least one blade.

Lifting his weapon, Drakkein looked down the scope and squeezed the trigger on his weapon with a light touch of his finger. A blue ball of light shot out of the barrel, joining two other balls of light as the other men fired their weapons. All three balls of light hit the reptile, which lifted its large head into the air and roared its displeasure.

It was pissed.

And it hadn't gone down.

The reptile spun in a sudden flurry of movement. Its four beady black eyes locked onto Drakkein and Staavo. Its forked tongue lashed out of its mouth before all four of its legs dug into the sand and launched itself at them.

"Get back!" Drakkein hollered as he aimed his rifle again and sent several blasts hurtling through the air and towards the reptile. A couple of the plasma bolts hit the reptile, but it didn't slow down as it snapped its jaw in anger.

Spinning on a boot, Drakkein darted after Staavo. As he ran, he heard Aknan firing from behind the reptile. It still wasn't going down, though. This scaly beast was too well protected.

Skidding to a sudden stop, Drakkein's feet threw up a wave of sand. Then he whipped out his long blade and turned back towards the reptile. Ducking low, he dodged the mouth of the reptile as it stormed up to him. As he ran underneath the belly, he raised his blade, and with both hands wrapped firmly around the hilt, he stabbed the blade into the soft flesh of the belly. Then he launched himself forward as he slid a gash through the belly. Green blood gushed out of the beast, covering his armor in the sticky fluid.

Drakkein yanked his blade out of the reptile and rolled out from underneath as the beast collapsed on the ground, thrashing in its final moments of life. Using a metal gloved hand, he wiped off the face screen of his helmet. There were still streaks of green running across the front of his helmet, but it was better than a sea of green blocking his view.

"Good job." Staavo remarked, "But maybe next time you should save some action for the rest of us."

Drakkein laughed. "Maybe you shouldn't have run away."

Staavo huffed some intelligible words.

"Now, we have to get this beast back to our butcher." Aknan kneeled beside the reptile and positioned a couple of devices below the reptile. Then he moved to the other side and positioned a couple more. "There, we should be able to move it now."

Drakkein pushed a few buttons on his wrist device, and slowly the devices Aknan placed under the reptile lifted the large beast and moved it towards the entrance to their underground city.

"Never enough for our growing population," Staavo said with eagerness to his voice.

A smile pulled up one corner of Drakkein's mouth. Staavo was the hunter of the group, always eager to join anyone who wanted to hunt.

"I'm just glad none us were injured."

"I'm amazed our shots didn't fell the beast," Aknan said as he shook his helmeted head. "All of us have good aim."

Drakkein shrugged. "Must be a more scaly beast than all the others we've hunted."

Even if it had been a bit more work, at least it would feed their people with some fresh meat.

The three of them followed the hovering reptile, and Drakkein's thoughts turned to the alien back in their hospital. Hopefully, by now, the alien would be conscious and feeling better. He was eager to satiate his curiosity and learn more about her people.

Chapter 6

Drakkein stared wide-eyed at the beauty before him.

The hospital staff had bathed her, wiped the sweat from her hair and body, and he found her… attractive. He felt a bit strange admitting to an attraction for an alien, but something about her size and vulnerability appealed to him.

The dainty alien woman laid on a medical bed, eyes closed, and very different than his people. Her blonde hair was so different than anyone in his city. All Aeci possessed black hair and silvery skin. The women tended to change the color of their hair and horns via dyes, but the men stuck to tattoos on their skin and horns to assert their independence.

Then his eyes drifted over the rest of her body, which was exposed to anyone's eyes who walked into the room. Her rosy nipples puckered tight in the cool air of the hospital, and his eyes skimmed over her smooth tummy to her belly button.

Then Drakkein's eyes skimmed further down until he reached the light curls that guarded her sex. His thoughts changed directions as he imagined this alien woman below him with lust clouding her eyes, and her lips parted in pleasure.

"She's stable."

Drakkein glanced up to see Ein enter the room. Her leathery wings held tightly against her back.

Her dark hair contained a purplish hue, and she wore gold bands on her grey horns. "She was severely dehydrated and burned by the sun, but some skin cream and an I.V. of water seem to have corrected any health issues. Again," Ein shrugged her shoulders, "we haven't dealt with her species before, so there could be other issues, but as far as we can tell, she should be healthy when she wakes."

"And when will she wake?" Drakkein turned his attention back to the blonde hair and alabaster skin, which almost blinded him as much as the sun would.

"Any time now," Ein said.

"I'll take her back to my place." And when he glanced up, he caught Ein shrugging.

"Whatever you want." Ein glanced at him over the medical bed. "Just be careful you don't startle her. We," she pointed to the wings behind her back, "don't exactly look like them."

"And her clothes?"

"They were too dirty for her healing skin, so we incinerated them. I can either give you something that the hospital has, or you can find something else for her to wear."

"I will find her something to wear," Drakkein promised as he scooped up the alien in his arms and lifted her off the bed. "If I need you…"

"You can call me day or night," Ein reassured him. "Even if it is just so she can see a female face."

Drakkein nodded before leaving the hospital with his alien woman and flying back to his home.

It didn't take him long to land on his personal balcony. Folding his wings against his back, he strode into his room. His people didn't see the need for windows, although some did have curtains on their balconies to prevent others from seeing in, but he'd had no need of curtains. It wasn't like he brought a lot of women home, and even if he did, he wasn't ashamed of someone seeing him pleasuring a woman.

Drakkein laid the alien on his bed, enjoying how she looked on his dark blue sheets. Her skin stood out in stark contrast, and he couldn't stop staring at her blonde locks. Sitting on the edge of the bed, he stroked a hand through her hair. The golden locks felt like the finest cloth, so soft and lustrous. If the green lights in his room had been brighter, he was sure it would reflect the light in shining glory.

Too bad all of their city was lit with green lights. The green felt better on their eyes, putting less strain on them, but it would never let her mass of golden hair shine like it could.

His hand seemed to have a mind of its own as it left her silky strands and moved to the soft, supple skin of her cheek. Her skin had lost its red hue, causing his slivery skin to stand out in contrast with her skin.

Whatever Ein had used to make the sunburn go away had been amazing. There wasn't a single pink tinge to any of her skin and no flaking of dead skin. Either the cream they'd used was a miracle, or they'd scrubbed the dead skin from her body.

One of his fingertips glided over a couple of small brown dots on her skin. He had no word for them. They were light in color and spread out over the tops of her cheeks and nose. Then his hand stroked down her neck, where he felt the pulse of the blood flowing through her. It was strong, like herself. Even when unconscious, she wasn't willing to let go of life.

His fingers smoothed over her delicate collar bone, and then his hand cupped the underside of one of her breasts.

Drakkein ground his teeth as his cock pushed painfully against his pants at its sudden eagerness. She might be different than himself, pale skin, no wings or horns, but he found her attractive.

He needed to stop.

The rosy bud on the tip of her breast hardened, poking straight up into the air in desperation of more contact like it begged him to shower it in attention.

"Mmmm." The Hazel murmured when she felt someone pinch her aching nipple between a couple of fingers. It felt so good. Better than good. It felt exquisitely painful and pleasurable at the same time.

Ever since landing on this planet with the rest of the colonists, she'd been pent up with no release. No one at the colony interested her, which meant her fingers had been her only sexual companions. As good as she was, it felt even better when all she had to do was relax and enjoy the pleasure washing over her. All she wanted now was relief. All she needed to know was that it wasn't Theo playing with her.

"Do you like this, female?" A deep dark voice growled between clenched teeth, and satisfaction filled her. It wasn't Theo, which meant she was ready to finally have an orgasm.

"Yes." Hazel breathed, though her eyes

hadn't opened.

She didn't want to open her eyes and ruin the fantasy of some strong, well-built man pleasuring her. If this was her imagination, it would wreck her, and if it wasn't… she didn't want to know which man in the colony pleased her this well.

Pinching her nipple, the man growled in pleasure when her back arched, shoving her breast fully into his hot hand.

"You know what I like?" She asked in a husky tone, hoping he was the kind of guy to enjoy her favorite form of pleasure.

"What's that?" He asked, his voice gone breathy.

"Your tongue on me." Hazel held her breath when his finger paused on her clit and nipple. Thrusting her hips up and down, she pumped his finger over her clit as she widened her thighs. "Your tongue on my clit."

"I can do that." The deep voice agreed.

The soft mattress shifted underneath her body as the man climbed onto the bed and positioned himself between her legs. His hands landed on the inside of her thighs, pushing them further apart, right before his hot breathed fanned out over her clit.

"You're so wet." He growled, seeming pleased with her body's reaction to him. "Glistening in invitation."

"I need a man."

Silence followed her words, and Hazel was tempted to crack open her eyes to see his reaction to her words.

But then he snarled, "You need me."

Then his mouth landed on her. He sucked her excited clit into his mouth, lightly scraping the bud with his teeth, and she squirmed under him with delight. Releasing her nub, he licked his tongue up and down her engorged lips before circling the tip of his tongue around her clit.

Oh, stars! Yes! This was exactly what she needed!

Hazel's hands found his head without her needing to open her eyes. She dug her fingers into the silky strands, and when her hands bumped into something hard on his head, she shoved aside the part of her mind that told her to look. She couldn't look. Not until she got what she needed.

If this ended… it would drive her insane. There'd been an itch for a few days now, and she really needed someone, other than Theo or her fingers, to scratch it for her.

With a growl, Drakkein ripped his mouth away from her tempting body and shoved himself off the bed. He couldn't believe how stirred up she got him. His cock raged within his pants, begging to be released and buried deep inside the woman on the bed. He wiped a hand down his smooth face, before glancing back at the woman on the bed, unable to resist.

His eyes widened, nearly jumping out of his eye sockets as he stared at her.

The woman's hand had found its way

between her creamy thighs, and if what he saw was correct, she pleasured herself… right there in front of him! Her body squirmed on the bed as she sought her release.

"Not without me." Drakkein groaned as he stripped his clothing off his body. His pants flew through the air, and before they could even hit the ground, his shirt followed swiftly after.

"You stopped, and I plan on finishing." The woman said matter of fact.

His wings flared out slightly as he stormed over to the bed. As he climbed onto the soft mattress, he positioned himself by her side, and with ease, knocked her thighs apart, revealing her enticing center to his gaze.

Sucking in a harsh breath, he took a second to watch the alien female pleasure herself. Thankfully, her sweet center looked the same as their women. Her finger swirled around a swollen nub right above her wet engorged folds.

"Is this what you like?" He asked breathlessly.

"Mmm, hmm."

Still, her eyes hadn't opened.

"I will get you to open your eyes." He promised.

"Perhaps." She challenged.

"Afraid I might be ugly?"

"Afraid you might not be real, and I don't want this to end before I come."

Drakkein's mouth curved up in a smile. He wasn't entirely sure how they understood each other, but his hard cock was his main focus. "Want me to play with you like that?"

"Yes." She said breathlessly.

"Then you have to open your eyes. I want you to see me." Drakkein couldn't start something with her, only to have her push him away when she realized he was an alien. An alien with large leathery wings and horns.

The woman huffed as she told him, "You better not be a dream."

"I'm not." He barely resisted telling her that he could make all her dreams come true, though.

Her eyes parted, and he found striking blue eyes looking back at him. He couldn't seem to drag his eyes away from those sky-blue eyes. To see that kind of color, he needed to be inside a suit on the surface of the planet, but here he was enjoying that color underground.

Drakkein froze, wondering what her reaction might be to him. He looked nothing like her. He sported a couple of horns atop his head and two leathery wings on his back, which he knew she could clearly see in the green lighting of his room.

But she didn't scream or yell. Her eyes widened slightly as her head cocked to the side as she studied him with her beautiful eyes. "Alien?"

Drakkein nodded as he prepared himself for her refusal. His cock would just have to go down. Not that it would. Not with images of her pleasuring herself on his bed floating through his mind.

Then the woman faintly shrugged one shoulder. "I like the horns. Kind of sexy."

She took a few more seconds, her eyes skimming over him, and he was happy to give her all the time she needed. When her eyes landed on his horns and wings, she seemed to take her time studying them. Seeming to come to a decision, the woman spread her creamy thighs and sent him a welcoming smile.

"I don't scare or shock you?" Drakkein wasn't sure why he wasn't jumping between her spread thighs, but he had to know.

"I've seen my fair share of aliens up there," she pointed to the ceiling of his room, but he knew she meant space, "and I can't say I've been with an alien, but I like what I see." Her eyes drifted over him, as she took in his chest and abs. "Really like what I see."

Reaching over her thigh, Drakkein knocked her hand away, replacing her finger with one of his own. Stroking the rough pad of his finger over her desire slicked nub, he felt his body stiffen as he fought the urge to straddle her and sink his cock into her soft entrance.

She moaned as her mouth opened, and her hips bucked. Her silky threads of hair flowed across his dark pillow as her head thrashed. "Feels so good." She purred. "You're so good."

"When was the last time you sought pleasure, female?" Drakkein's finger circled around her nub faster as her bucks grew more desperate.

Then her thighs clamped down around his hand, and her head shot off the pillow as she shattered around his hand.

"Yes!" She screamed before her head landed back against the pillow with a soft thud.

The tip of his cock bumped up against the outside of her calf, and her head shot back up as her gaze zeroed in on him. "I want you inside me."

With his cock throbbing in need, Drakkein couldn't say no to her, nor did he wish to say no.

Scooting forward on the bed, he leaned over her, placing his hands beside each of her shoulders and his legs between her soft thighs. Her blue eyes skimmed over his face, their depths hazy with her desire. His cock strained towards her hot center.

"I want to be inside you."

"Yes." She spread her legs wider, lifting her feet slightly until her heels dug into the flesh of his thighs. "I want you inside me."

He was about to take an alien woman. He faltered as he looked down at her. "I'm an alien." He said, feeling stupid with each word. They'd already discussed him being an alien.

"Clearly." She responded with a light chuckle.

Still, he wasn't sure he should take her. He'd brought her back to learn more about her people, not learn more about her body. He should be treating her like an ambassador, not a woman who called to something inside him.

As if sensing his hesitation, she lifted her hips, brushing the tip of his cock against her sweet wet core.

Drakkein shuddered as all thought left his mind in a rush. Putting weight on one hand, he gripped his cock with the other and positioned it at her entrance. Slowly, he slid the head of his cock into her, and she felt so velvety smooth. She welcomed him with a tight clutch of warmth.

The woman's hands rubbed the muscles of his shoulders and back as she clawed at him with her desire. She didn't mark his skin with her nails. Instead, her touch was light as she only used her fingertips to explore his back. When her hands bumped into his wings, she skirted past them without a care.

As Drakkein sank into her, he bumped into something. A bead of sweat collected between his shoulder blades as he paused. Maybe their people weren't compatible after all.

"Is that all?" She asked with a raised eyebrow. Disappointment shone bright in her swirling blue eyes.

Drakkein shook his head as he chuckled. "That is not all. It's just the tip." Placing his other hand back on the bed beside her, he thrust his cock deep inside her, breaking past the barrier and hoping they were compatible, and he wouldn't harm her while making love.

He heard her gasp, but his cock and instinct drove him. Her hands clenched on his shoulders, the nails digging into his flesh. He pumped into her. Every thrust deep and long, and within no time, her hands once more roamed across his muscles as he sought their joined release.

Rearing back, Drakkein grabbed a hold of her waist as he lifted her hips off the bed and drove into her warmth like a savage beast bent on claiming her body for his own. Any man before him would be forgotten, and she would never dream of another man.

Only him.

She was his.

Watching her face, pleasure rolled through him to see a delicate blush tainting her cheeks as her mouth opened, and her hands fell onto the bed and gripped the sheets in tight fists.

The woman cried out as her hands came up to press her breasts together. Her fingers teased her nipples, but he felt like she teased him. From this angle, he looked down her body to the valley of her breasts. All he could think about was thrusting his cock between her breasts. Next time, he promised himself. Next time.

Then her cries turned to whimpers as he felt her slick entrance clench down around him.

"Are you coming?"

Her blonde head of hair thrashed across his pillow as she shook her head. "So close… so close." She panted.

Pressure built at the base of his cock. "I'm going to come inside you." He ground out as his jaw clenched, and his balls tightened.

The woman's hands roamed all over his shoulders and slowly dipped until she ran her fingertips down his chest. He loved the feel of her fingers running over his sweat-slicked skin.

"Yes!" Drakkein roared to his ceiling as he threw back his head and drove into her. His balls tightened before pumping his hot seed deep into her tight sheath. His head threw forward, and he watched as the woman before him shattered.

"Ahh!" She moaned under him as her body squeezed his cock, drawing out every last drop of seed he had to offer.

He thrust into her until her body collapsed back onto the bed.

Drakkein collapsed off to the side, his cock sliding free from her warmth. Reaching out, he scooped her up and brought her into his chest. It'd been a long time since he'd found a woman who could draw out such a mindless climax from him. It left him wondering if it was because she was a novelty.

Chapter 7

Hazel cuddled up closer to the man's chest. He was so warm, and she felt certain she could remain in his arms for the rest of her life. Snuggling her head closer to his chest, she sucked in his spicy male scent. He smelled like comfort, no matter how crazy that made her sound.

Something leathery touched her back, and Hazel cracked an eye to spot a large black wing curved above her.

What?

"Oh, my stars!" Hazel bolted up in the bed, and her eyes landed on the alien lying beside her. A horned, winged alien! "No, I did not!" She shoved herself off the bed. "I can't believe myself." She slammed her hands across her cheeks as mortification overwhelmed her.

"Why don't you come back to bed?" The alien male's gravelly voice rolled over her, sending goosebumps of pleasure racing over her skin. He patted the mattress invitingly.

"What? No way!" Hazel glanced down and found herself butt naked. Slamming an arm across her breasts and a hand over her light curls, she did her best to protect herself from view.

The alien chuckled in a deep voice that sent thrills racing across her skin in the form of goosebumps.

"I think covering yourself is a bit foolish after what we just shared." He rubbed a hand on the dark cover, then paused and held up a hand as he rubbed two fingers together. "Is this blood?"

Shame and embarrassment warmed Hazel's cheeks. "I can't believe this." She'd found the aliens, and then promptly slept with one of them. She didn't regret it, because from what she remembered, it had been fun and pleasurable. Her cheeks warmed more, but this time in excitement as flashes of their time together played through her mind.

He glanced up at her with a raised eyebrow. "Is this blood?"

He didn't know about virgins?

She wasn't about to be the one to give him a biology lesson.

The alien rose from the bed, and a skitter entered her heart. He was tall. Like giant type of tall. Okay, she was running away with herself, but he was still a couple heads taller than herself. And those wings. Her eyes widened as she took in the width of his leathery wings. Each wing was tipped with a decent sized black claw, and then there were those horns that shot out from his temple and up into the air.

Hazel squinted in the green light of the room. Were those tattoos on his horns?

He made for an impressive sight.

Although rumors in the colony had been off about his kind, they hadn't been far off the truth. The man in front of her sent a thrill of fear spiking through her, but she held her ground.

"I don't know." She shrugged.

In the blink of an eye, he had her pinned up

against one of the stone walls. "Is this blood?" He raised his hand to her view.

Hazel glanced down at his fingers as more heat pumped into her cheeks. It wasn't like his fingertips were soaked in blood, but she did see the crimson liquid smeared across the silvery grey skin.

"Yes." She whispered.

"I hurt you?" The alien backed away from her, looking stunned as he stared at his fingers.

She took a brief second to let her eyes roam over the man in front of her. He was bare to her view, and the sight of his well-built body had her responding with a flood of wetness between her thighs. Her eyes dipped further to his cock. It wasn't hard, but it was still a good size and pleasured her well a few hours ago.

Then her eyes drifted back up to his face, where he still looked traumatized by her blood on his fingers.

With an internal sigh, she took pity on the poor alien man.

"Well," Hazel reached a hand behind her head and scratched her neck as she tried to come up with a way to say this, "don't your people have… virgins?"

"Vir…gins?"

"Human women, like me," she pointed to her chest, "we have an inner barrier until our first time."

"Our women don't have this." The alien shook his horned head. "I am your first lover?" A cocky smile grew on his lips.

Hazel rolled her eyes. "I know! I know!" She raised her hands to her burning cheeks. "It's weird these days to save your virginity. Here in the space age, no one thinks about saving it for marriage, but I guess I have an antiquated mind. I always thought I'd save myself for my husband." If her cheeks burned any hotter, she was sure she'd be on fire.

The alien chuckled. "It would be strange in our culture as well. We usually have several partners before settling down."

"Same for us." Hazel glanced around. "Where are my clothes?"

"The hospital took them."

"Hospital?" How long had she been out? She didn't remember a hospital.

"Come," the alien motioned for her to follow him as he walked up to a metal dresser. "There is a lot to tell you." He began shuffling through the drawers. "We found you out in the desert by yourself. You fell unconscious, so we brought you back here to our city."

"And," Hazel coughed, "how did I end up in your bed." And how did she end up there in the future? Oh, dear. One time in his bed and she already wanted there to be another time. Her father would give her a good talking to when he found out about this. They had come to this planet to escape alien complications and Earth meddling in peoples' affairs, and here she couldn't resist getting intimate with the people burning their crops. Talk about complications.

The alien shrugged his broad shoulders. "I figured my bed would be more comfortable than the hospital bed."

Too comfortable, in her opinion.

From this angle, Hazel had a good view of the alien's wings. They were large and folded up behind him. She wanted to reach out and stroke a hand down one to see if it would feel like leather, but she kept her hands firmly beside her. She had no idea how he would react to her stroking his wings.

"Here," the alien spun around and presented her with folded clothing.

"Thanks." Hazel kept her eyes down, looking towards the ground. She felt awkward being around him. She didn't know why, but she wasn't sure how to act around her first lover. Scurrying back over to the bed, she laid out the clothes. "You don't happen to have a bra and panty set, do you?" She glanced over her shoulder to find the alien dressed in a pair of black pants, leaving his drool-worthy torso bare. That would be a distraction.

"If you're talking about those little undergarments you wore, then no. My people don't have those." He winked. "Less clothing between our bodies when we want to share pleasure together."

Hazel's cheeks flamed even more as she quickly faced back to her clothes and slipped them on. A bit of jealousy inched into her heart that he would have women's clothing in his dresser. Clearly, she wasn't the first woman to need a pair of clothing after sleeping with him.

With a huff of irritation at her jealousy, she slipped the shirt over her head before facing him again.

"I don't know what came over us…" she waved her hand in the air, "earlier, but let me restart this properly." Hazel stuck her hand out. "I'm Hazel, and I come from the human colony on the surface."

The alien glanced at her outstretched hand.

"Oh, silly me." Hazel laughed lightly. "In my culture, we shake hands with someone we've just met."

"Ah," the alien held out a hand, she grabbed a hold of it and shook it firmly. "I am Drakkein from the Aeci colony."

"Aeci." She repeated. Then she caught the last word. "Colony?" She raised her eyes until she met his dark grey eyes.

"We are a colony like yourselves."

Hazel's head shot back as her eyes widened. "We assumed you were native to the planet."

"We arrived here a couple of generations ago. Our planet underwent a governmental change, and not everyone agreed with the new laws and reforms, so we took several ships and went in search for a new home."

"Sounds very similar to the reasons we landed here." Hazel smiled. Maybe if she could get everyone to recognize how similar they were, their people could live in harmony on this small desert planet. "Do you think I could speak with your leader?"

A knock sounded on the only door to the room. Then a woman's head popped into the room as the door was cracked open, "Drakkein? I thought I heard some noises coming from in here."

From where Hazel stood, the woman would have to crane her neck to see Hazel, so she got her chance to studying the alien woman without being noticed. Just like Drakkein, the woman had two horns atop her head, but unlike Drakkein, her horns were tinged with purple on the tips.

"We are fine."

"We?" The woman glanced around until her dark eyes landed on Hazel. "What… what is she?" The woman's eyes grew wide as they skimmed over Hazel.

"Hello." Hazel smiled with a small wave. "I'm Hazel."

The woman's mouth dropped. "She speaks our language?!"

"Umm, no, I don't." Hazel clarified. "Most of my people have a chip behind their ear," she pointed to right behind her ear, "something we are usually given at birth, and it translates most languages." Thankfully, it appeared to have no issue with whatever language these people spoke.

"I don't understand." The woman shook her head as she looked back at Drakkein for answers. "Why is there an alien in your room?"

Alien.

Hazel frowned, and then nodded her head. She supposed, right now, among these people, she was the alien.

"Ola, this doesn't concern you. Leave."

Ola's eyes narrowed on Drakkein before she tossed Hazel one last hostile glance and left, closing the door behind her.

"Who was that?" Hazel hitched a thumb at the now closed door.

"My nosy housemaid," Drakkein said as he approached her with slow, steady steps.

Hazel backed up a couple of steps, and he froze.

His dark, almost black eyes pierced her. "Do I scare you?"

"Honestly?"

He nodded his horned head.

"I wouldn't say you scare me." Hazel hedged, trying to be diplomatic. She'd already been unprofessional and slept with one of the aliens. She was here to discuss terms for peace between their people, and so far, all she'd done was almost die in the desert and sleep with the first alien she'd come across. "I just haven't seen an… Aeci before, and you do look intimidating. Right, Aeci? That's how you say it?"

"Aeci, yes." Drakkein stepped closer, and this time she didn't move backward. "Our leader, Briktox, has been informed about your arrival. He is busy, but he thought it might be good for you to see our colony before we discuss anything, so you can see how we live and what we value."

"Oh." Hazel nodded her head.

She was a bit nervous about traipsing around an alien colony, but at the same time, it thrilled her. It was the first exciting thing to happen since she'd arrived here with her father… and she liked it. She kind of missed a bit of excitement in her life. There were no clubs, no aliens, nothing but animal chores, and fending off Theo's attentions.

"Are we going out now?"

He nodded his head.

"Umm, aren't you forgetting something?"

Drakkein cocked his head to the side as his dark eyes skimmed over her and then glanced around the room with a shrug. "What am I forgetting?"

"You don't have a shirt on." Hazel pointed to his bare and distracting torso.

A saucy smile spread over his grey lips as he winked at her. "Want me to cover this up so you can focus on our colony?"

Hazel felt cornered here. If she said yes, it meant his chest distracted her, and if she said no, he wouldn't put on a shirt, and she could be distracted while they toured the colony.

"Not at all." Hazel lied, deciding to go with what she thought was the better of the two options. "Please, show the way." She waved a hand towards the door.

"Follow me then." Drakkein strode past her, away from the only door in the room.

Frowning, Hazel followed after him as he walked towards his balcony, his balcony without a railing. Eyes widening, she took a couple steps onto the balcony before letting out a random little noise of surprise.

This wasn't a colony. This was a city!

Glancing to her left, Hazel saw green lights shining out of several buildings. They weren't really buildings, but she lacked the right word. It was like his people had carved out a canyon under the surface, and then carved out homes and buildings from the rock walls. Then she looked to the right and saw the same. It stretched on and on, even further than her eye could see.

"Wow."

"Impressive, is it not?"

She glanced over at Drakkein, who stood with his chest puffed out as he surveyed the city around him with his hands on his hips. He was proud of what they had created, and he had every right to be. This was so much more spectacular than what her people had set up on the surface.

"How long did it take your people to create this?"

"Many years," Drakkein said honestly. "And it isn't perfect. We've had a few sections collapse on us, but I was a child when the last one happened and don't remember it too well."

"Did anyone…?" Hazel grimaced.

"We lost a couple of people," he hesitated slightly before saying, "my mother included."

Hazel grimaced even more. Out of everyone in their colony, she shouldn't have been the one to come and speak with the Aeci. She had no tact, and now she was in a situation where she had no idea what to say.

"I'm sorry." It sounded lame, even to her ears. "I could never imagine losing my mother."

Drakkein turned to face her. "The part that hurts me the worst is the fact I was so young that I have no memories of her to mourn. I can barely make out her face, and I have no idea what her voice was like."

"No pictures?"

He shook his head. "None. My mother and father weren't much into documenting their lives."

Hazel nodded her head. She understood his emotions, but what was she supposed to say now?! She racked her brain for something to say but came up empty. So, she stood there in silence, picking at her fingernails while they both watched life in the colony zip by on leathery wings.

The Aeci flew from place to place.

It blew her mind. It had to be absolutely thrilling to feel the air whip by their face, through their hair, and to flap those large leathery black wings.

"What would you like to see first?" Drakkein asked her.

"Oh, gosh." Her tummy took that moment to rumble. "How about some food?"

A smile broke out over his lips once more, and it shocked the breath from her lungs. He was stunning. Those sharp angles of his jawline, the nose that had healed improperly after a break, and those dark eyes that were both dangerous and filled to the brim with light. He must break a million hearts a day.

"I know the perfect place for some food. If you can't find something there, you won't find anything anywhere else." Drakkein slashed his hand through the air as he moved closer to her. "You'll want to stand in front of me."

"Why?" Hazel asked, as a bit of suspicion had her eyes narrowing on him.

"Otherwise, I can carry you in my arms like a child." He held out his ripped arms.

She had to refrain from squealing like a kid excited about some candy. She should have told him to wear a shirt, but she wasn't about to say it now. The moment had passed, and he would just give her another sexy smile. They may not have known each other long, but she felt like she knew his personality already.

Shrugging, Hazel stepped in front of him, her back to him. The moment he stepped up behind her, she found the air zip with electricity at his presence, and her body warmed at the memories of what they'd done in bed together.

Drakkein's strong arms wrapped around her waist, and his head dipped down until his lips rested right up against her ear. "Make sure you hold on tight."

"Okay?"

Something snapped behind them, and then Drakkein's legs bent, and then they leaped over the edge of the balcony. Her eyes widened as she saw how far up they were, and how far away the ground was, but then a smile spread over her lips. The drop stole her breath. Otherwise, she would have screamed in excitement.

Now, this was thrilling!

Chapter 8

Drakkein wasn't sure whether she was scared speechless or having a grand time as they plummeted through the air. Lights and sights blew past them in a blur, until finally, he spread his wings wide, and they gently soared through the air.

He hoped his little alien thought this was exciting, because he could never get enough of soaring through the air, and he wanted to share this small joy with her.

When Drakkein spotted the balcony he wanted to land on, he tipped his wings slightly, slowing them down. Shifting his body, he positioned their feet so they would land on the balcony. As they landed, he made sure to keep her feet up, so he took the brunt of the landing.

Once steady, Drakkein released his hold on her, allowing her to walk a couple of steps away from him.

Hazel spun around, a smile plastered all over her face, and her sky blue eyes danced with joy. "That was amazing! I've never done something like that before!"

"I'm glad you enjoyed it." Drakkein chuckled. "Flying is something I've always enjoyed. Something about it that frees the soul."

"I did notice," she mentioned as they stood there on the balcony, "that there are stairs and bridges.

Why didn't we just take those down here?"

"It would have taken much longer. We flew about thirty flights down and five buildings over." Drakkein turned to glance up at where they'd flown from. "I wouldn't even be able to pick my home out from here."

"Faster to fly than to walk. Got it."

When he turned to face Hazel, she gave him a thumbs up and a smile. He wasn't familiar with the gesture, but it seemed positive.

"Come," Drakkein placed a hand to the small of her back and guided her beside him. "Food is just a door away."

"Yum."

As they approached a purplish metal door, it slid open to reveal a long wide corridor filled to the brim with stalls and people.

"You can find anything here." He waved an arm to encompass the large area.

"Wow," Hazel said from beside him as her eyes bugged out of her face.

He didn't know this woman, but already he found pleasure in her reactions. Every emotion she felt was right there for the people around her to see.

"Am I safe?" She turned her sweet face up to him, her eyes searching for reassurance.

"Our people will be curious, as would be expected, but no one here means you any harm," Drakkein said as he surveyed the Aeci who manned and viewed the stalls of food.

"What about…" Hazel trailed off as she wrung her hands in front of her. "What about the Aeci my people killed? I assume he has family. They may not enjoy me being here."

Drakkein paused. He hadn't thought about that. The young man's family might want retribution for their family member's death. Still, the probability of running into one of them would be low… he hoped. Their colony was more like a city these days, with a lot of people, and he was sure word hadn't yet spread about Hazel's arrival.

"I will defend you." He held a hand up to his bare chest as his wings flared behind him protectively.

Hazel's eyes narrowed on him. "Not sure that really makes me any more comfortable."

Drakkein glowered down at her. She doubted his ability to keep her safe, and it… bothered him. A lot. He wanted her to believe in him.

"It's not an insult to you." Hazel quickly added as she reached out a hand and laid it softly on his lower arm. A jolt of desire shot through him at the simple touch as she continued, "There are just a lot more people. If they swarm us, you'd have no chance."

"No one here is looking for a fight." Drakkein was sure of that much when it came to his people. "We came here to escape fighting and persecution." When he saw her mouth open, he held up a hand, "But that doesn't mean we won't defend what we made on this planet." He smiled at her, "We should discuss things on a full stomach. Feel free to lead the way, I will be right behind you."

"Okay." A light blush crept across her cheeks as her blue eyes danced with excitement. "Where to start?"

Drakkein knew the question wasn't for him, but for her as she tried to take in the hundreds of stalls set up before her. He'd lived here his entire life, and he still wasn't sure he'd eaten at every single one yet.

"I guess I should just choose one and go from there, right?" Hazel turned her striking blue eyes on him, and he found himself lost for words, so he nodded dumbly in answer. Those eyes. He might never be able to enjoy a blue sky without a suit on, but at least when he looked into her eyes, he could never forget how stunning it would be.

Hazel stepped forward and wandered to the first stall. People standing in line caught sight of her and spun around to gawk.

When their eyes raised to him in question, he kept his face straight and placed a protective hand to her lower back. She seemed so interested in the stall that she hadn't noticed the crowd around her as his people tried to get their first view of an alien. It had been generations since his people traveled through space, so most people had no idea what to make of her.

"I can't read any of the words on the sign, what does it say?"

Drakkein cast his eyes up to the sign that had words backlit by green lights. "It says they offer several preparations of grakid."

"Graw-kid?" Hazel asked as she turned those eyes on him.

Drakkein would have to blind himself… every time those eyes focused on him, he wanted to melt into a giant puddle. "The giant reptiles roaming the surface of the planet."

"What?!" She looked repulsed for a second, before she slowly nodded her head, as though she warmed to the idea. "Is it good?"

"It's one of our favorites."

"I'd like some of that then."

"You don't look so sure about it."

Hazel shrugged. "Like you said, I should experience your culture and see how you live. How can I do that if I don't live like you?"

"I'll get us some then." Drakkein stepped up to the counter of the stall. "Two of the seared grakid."

"Coming up." The woman behind the counter said as she put in the order, but she couldn't seem to drag her dark eyes away from Hazel. "Is that one of the aliens from the surface?" She raised a grey-skinned hand to briefly point at Hazel.

"It is."

"What is she doing down here?" The woman's silver eyebrows shot together as she continued to stare at Hazel.

Drakkein opened his mouth but snapped it closed. He wasn't entirely sure what Hazel's motives were, but he had a guess, "She is here to speak with my father about the tensions between our people. The surface aliens appear to want peace with us."

"That would be nice." The woman's silver lips spread into a smile as she nodded her head happily. "I think most of us would like peace with the aliens."

"I am hoping we can find peace as well." Drakkein looked over at the human woman who stared around their home in wonderment. He'd even like it if she could stay so he could continue to stare into those gorgeous sky blue eyes.

"Here you are," Drakkein offered her a stick with chunks of steaming white meat on it.

"Ooooo." Hazel licked her lips as she eagerly took the offered stick with both of her hands. "It smells good." Better than she would have expected roasted lizard to smell.

"Tastes even better." He promised her as he took a bite of his own meat stick. "Mmmm." He murmured as he chewed his bite and sent her a wink.

Taking a deep breath, Hazel bent her head to the side as she took a bite out of the topmost chunk of lizard meat. As she chewed, she nodded her head with pursed lips. The lizard creature was pretty good. It was lean, with a slightly gamey taste, but not overwhelming. The spices on the meat

Holding a hand up to her mouth, Hazel said, "I'm surprised we never thought about catching and eating these Grakids." It would solve some of their issues with food reserves, and she was sure her people would rather eat lizard than nothing.

"They aren't easy to kill, and we've lost several men over the years, but if you can manage to kill them, they provide a lot of meat."

"Maybe you could teach my people how to hunt them someday." She suggested, testing the waters for how he might feel about helping her people stay alive.

"Perhaps." He agreed as he gobbled down his stick of meat and then threw the stick into a trash can.

Hazel quickly ate the rest of her lizard meat,

and then flicked the stick into the trash… and then she noticed the attention she'd garnered. Aeci stood around her, their dark eyes wide as they studied her.

"I seem to be quite popular," Hazel remarked, a bit disturbed by the attention, but also hoping this would be good for their two people. It would be good for them to grow used to seeing each other.

One of Drakkein's leather wings flicked out, protecting her back as he took a more protective stance next to her. Some of the people quickly shook their horned heads and walked away, but others continued to stare unabashedly.

Slowly, Drakkein got them moving again, and now she had a good chance at studying the Aeci and their massive colony.

All of them had horns and wings, but the women possessed slightly smaller horns, which most of them had decorated by dyeing with different colors. A popular color seemed to be dyeing the tips in a dark purple, while others had gone for gold. Other women had chosen to use bracelets to glam up their horns. The women were also daintier than their male counterparts. The women were about her size, which made her feel a bit better. At least she wasn't the shortest one in their colony.

Hazel caught a scent that had her mouth drooling. "What is that?" She said, hoping Drakkein would know of what she spoke.

Lifting his nose into the air, he took a whiff and then smiled. "One of my favorites." He winked at her as he guided her over to another stall, his wing still outstretched behind her. "This is my favorite dessert."

They lined up behind a couple of Aeci.

"Why did your people choose to move here?" Drakkein glanced down at her.

Hazel laughed as she said, "We thought no one else would want to move onto a desert planet." She shrugged. "We figured it would be a hard place to live, but no one would ever come and uproot us because there were no valuable resources here."

Drakkein chuckled. "We too thought people would stay away, but you proved us wrong."

They moved forward in line as someone stepped out of line after placing their order.

"My father started a colonist group looking to get away from our home planet, Earth, and the troubles of space… and aliens." Hazel rolled her eyes. "The colonists were just looking for a peaceful place without a lot of excitement and complications."

"Then, it sounds like your people would be interested in solving this peacefully," Drakkein said, and she saw him studying her with those dark eyes.

"I hope so."

His eyes narrowed on her, and she wondered what he'd caught until he asked, "Do they know you're here?"

"They've probably found me missing, so yes?" Hazel figured the moment they found her missing, her father would know exactly where she'd gone. She had made her opinions on peace clear before leaving.

"I was wondering about your people. To send a lone woman into an alien colony seems foolish and risky. There's no way they could be assured of your safety unless they thought you were expendable." He growled the last word like it would piss him off if her people thought she was disposable.

"No," she shook her head, causing her hair to swirl around her shoulders, "I am the foolish one, but I want there to be peace. Everyone else is nervous now that your people have burned our crops, and they are unsure how to react."

"We didn't start it." He reminded her.

Oh, she knew. And she still could scarcely believe what those idiots had done. For a bunch of colonists trying to escape complications, they sure had created some serious issues.

Drakkein's eyes just stared at her, unnerving her, since she couldn't read a single emotion on his stone like face. Gosh, he'd be good at a gambling house. He'd probably rake in millions of credits with ease with that straight face.

They stepped up to the counter as the last person in front of them stepped off to the side.

"Hello," the woman at the counter said, as she looked at the screen in front of her, and when her head rose, her eyes widened as she took in Hazel. Then she looked up at Drakkein. "Who… what… is this?" She pointed a silver-skinned finger at Hazel.

"An alien from the colony on the surface." Drakkein supplied.

"What is she doing here?"

"Ordering some food." Drakkein raised a brow at the woman across the counter from them.

"O—of course." She stammered as she shook the shock from her face. "What can I get you two?"

"We will take a couple orders of the fruute."

"Is that all?"

"It is."

Hazel watched him pay, and then the woman turned, grabbed a couple items, and handed him two small brown bags.

After taking the items, Drakkein once more guided Hazel away from the counter with his wing and hand at the small of her back. Then he wrapped his other wing around her as they stopped, hiding them from the view of prying eyes.

"A little intimate." Hazel joked as she laughed lightly. A strange flutter of excitement soared through her as he surrounded her fully. She never thought she would find a man with horns and wings attractive, but hot damn. She wished they were back in his room so she could entice him again.

"I don't want my people interrupting us while you enjoy what I think," he held a hand up to his bare pec, "is the best dessert my people have to offer."

"Oooo." Hazel clapped her hands in front of her face. "Now you've got me excited. I have a major sweet tooth." She patted her tummy. "Maybe too much of a sweet tooth."

Drakkein passed her one of the bags, and as she took it from him, her fingers brushed his silver-skinned hand. A sizzle sparked in her as her body reacted to the memories of their first encounter.

"Thanks." She whispered breathlessly as she peeled back the folded bag. Peering into the bag, her mouth watered when she found a crispy pastry staring right back at her. Reaching a hand into the bag, she drew out the small pastry, and eagerly she took a bite. The crisp pastry flaked in her mouth, and a dense nutty filling teased her taste buds.

"Oh yeah," Hazel held up a hand to her mouth as she talked over her mouthful of food. "This is fantastic." With the rationing at the colony, she hadn't eaten a sweet since leaving space behind. She would need to have her father negotiate some of these when they sought peace.

With a couple more bites, each of them finished their sweet morsels.

Hazel wasn't ashamed of licking the grease off her fingers.

"No need to eat your fingers. I can order a couple more."

Hazel didn't miss the twinkle in his dark eyes.

Drakkein took the empty bag from her before reaching a hand behind her head, gripping the back of her skull, and slanting his lips over hers.

Stunned, Hazel stood there like a tree, until her brain caught up, and then she melted. In the privacy of his wings, she eagerly met his searching lips as her hands came up to caress the hard muscles of his chest.

Oh yeah.

She wasn't sure which was better. The melt-in-her-mouth dessert or Drakkein kissing her.

Despite having just eaten a dessert, he tasted spicy and warm. Their lips melded together so well, and she felt helpless to resist, not that she would. She'd never found a guy who could kiss her like this.

An ache entered her heart, and someday she would have to return to her people and leave him behind. Ugh. Her heart broke in her chest as she returned every kiss. If she had to leave this behind, then she would enjoy every moment.

Drakkein broke away, their mouths inches apart. He placed a tender light kiss on her lips and then pulled back fully. "I find you hard to resist human.

Woah.

Her heart thundered in her chest as she tried to catch her breath. "Same here, Aeci." Her words were breathless with a bit of a pant.

"When you're ready, we can continue through the market."

"I think," Hazel took a breath, "I'm ready to start talking about peace and to your leader."

The faster she got the talks started, the sooner she could let her father know she wasn't dead. Her father wouldn't be pleased to know she'd come here, but she hadn't felt like there was any other option left to her. Their colony was based on peace, and they weren't off to a great start. Instead, they'd started drama on a planet they couldn't leave.

Drakkein nodded his head. "Let us head out to do that then."

Chapter 9

With her pulse racing and a bead of sweat trickling down her back, Hazel walked over to the balcony with Drakkein. Now came the hardest part of her mission, trying to make peace after her people killed one of the Aeci. She wasn't exactly sure what she could offer to appease the loss of a life. She wasn't sure there was anything she could give them in return for the life taken. All she could do was hope the Aeci leader knew what he'd want.

"Ready?" Drakkein stepped up behind her and wrapped his strong arms of steel around her middle.

Raising her hands and clutching those arms, she nodded her head, "Yes."

She heard Drakkein whip out his leathery wings with a snap, and then with a couple strong flaps, they soared up and into the air. Green lights zipped by them as cold air from being underground pinched her face as the zoomed through the air.

The purplish metal interspersed with the rock walls they'd used to form their colony were beautiful. The green lights were a bit odd and creepy, but she figured she had plenty of time to ask Drakkein all about his world and why they did certain things the way they did.

As they approached a waterfall, a roar filled her ears as the rushing water plummeted further into the planet.

So, the planet did have water!

This discovery of hers could help her people. All she had to do was again figure out what her people could offer the Aeci in return for some of the life-giving water.

Drakkein's wings flapped by his side as he halted their speed and landed on a balcony with a slight bump. Once he released his hold on her, she stepped away and pointed to the waterfall.

"The planet has water?"

"It does, but good luck reaching the water from the surface or even detecting it." Drakkein glanced over at the roaring wall of water. "The surface of the planet doesn't allow scans to penetrate, and it's only in isolated pockets around the world."

Maybe she could initiate trade between their people. She would have to figure out what they could offer the Aeci, but she was sure they could come up with something. There was always something that someone else would want.

"This way." Drakkein placed a hand to the small of her back and guided her back behind the rushing wall of water, where a corridor of purplish metal buried deep into the stone of the planet.

Trusting Drakkein, Hazel walked confidently beside him. In the green light of the corridor, she snuck a peek at her clothing. It was basic, nothing fancy, and she grew a bit nervous she might be underdressed for a meeting with the Aeci leader. Nothing she could do about it now though.

She picked anxiously at the loose-fitting clothing, wishing there was some way for her to improve it on the fly, but she came up with nothing and soon abandoned picking at her clothes.

They broke into a decent sized chamber with a woman sitting at a metal desk. She twirled a lock of her dyed pink hair around a silver-skinned finger. So far, coloring their hair and horns seemed to be a cultural trait in the Aeci, because Hazel wasn't about to believe the pink strands were natural.

Casting her eyes up when she heard their boots on the metal floor, the Aeci woman's eyes flickered over Drakkein and his bare chest, and Hazel saw a flicker of appreciation spark in the other woman's eyes.

A surge of jealousy rose up inside in her chest, but Hazel quickly shut it down.

She wasn't here to get tangled up in a sticky inter-species relationship. She was here to make peace and allow their two people to live in harmony. Nothing more. Nothing more!

Then the Aeci woman glanced at her, and she raised a matching pink eyebrow. Turning her attention back to Drakkein she asked, "Do you have an appointment?"

"No, but my father will want to speak with the human."

The human.

The phrasing of his words stung a bit. He could have introduced her with her name, which he knew, and then said she was human. He didn't have to strictly call her "the human". It shouldn't bother her, but no matter how many times she chanted that in her head, she couldn't get the sting of hurt to leave her alone.

"Let me make sure he has time." The woman's dark eyes turned back to the screen on her desk, and her fingers danced across it before she raised her head with a smile on her lips. "He will see you." She waved a hand towards a purplish metal door that slid open.

"Time to see my father, Hazel." Drakkein pushed her towards the open door with a hand to the small of her back.

Taking deep even breathes, Hazel prepared herself. She wasn't sure what to expect at the end of this corridor. She was sure Drakkien's father would look like him, with wings and horns, she just wasn't sure what kind of personality he would have. Hopefully, he was open-minded.

They walked into a small chamber where a man sat behind a massive metal desk. His wings were flared out in what had to be a relaxed position for him. He looked up, and a smile creased his lips, lines forming in his silver skin. He looked like an older version of Drakkein, which was good news for Drakkein, because his father was handsome.

"Father."

Hazel glanced at Drakkein to see his head bowed ever so slightly.

"Drakkein." His father bowed his head in return. "I've heard of this woman who you have brought back." His father turned his attention to Hazel. His dark eyes glistened with curiosity.

The bottom tip of Drakkein's wing prodded her butt with a sharp poke.

"Hello, sir." Hazel rushed to jump into the conversation. "I am Hazel Clarke, and I've come from the human colony on the surface." Some of that was kind of obvious, but she figured too much information was better than too little.

"I am Zodur, the leader of the Aeci, and," he motioned a hand to Drakkein, "his father."

"I gathered." Hazel smiled at him.

Zodur rose from his seat, and like his son, he towered over anyone her size. His leather wings pulled up tightly behind his back, just the tips showing above his shoulders, the curved clawed tip. And, of course, he sported a pair of black horns atop his temple.

"Why have you come here?" Zodur asked as he strode around the table and leaned a hip against an edge of the metal desk.

Hazel folded her hands in front of her. Here went nothing. "Our people are coming to blows, and I'm hoping we can find a way towards a peaceful resolution. Both of our people chose to live here on this desert planet, and I don't think either of us intends to leave."

Her people couldn't leave, but she wasn't about to say that to him. It was more of a weakness than a strength, and she didn't need to go around spilling her colony's vulnerabilities.

Zodur nodded his head as he rested his hands on his hips. "Your people killed one of our own."

"I realize that." And here was the hard part. How could she possibly make up for the loss of life? "I'm here to discuss terms for peace to prevent any further deaths from occurring. If there's a way to live in harmony, I'm sure both colonies," she looked over her shoulder to Drakkein, "would be willing to work towards that goal." She glanced back at Zodur.

"I am sure my people would also want peace, but I have to show them that the death of one of ours won't go unpunished."

"I'm here to listen to ideas." Hazel waved her hands at her side.

"Now that I know your people would be willing to work out peace, I will have to discuss with the family of the deceased to see what would work for them. I can tell you they will want justice, most likely some sort of incarceration for the offenders."

Hazel nodded her head. "Of course. Whatever you come up with will have to be discussed and agreed upon with my people."

"It's settled then." Zodur glanced away from her and over to Drakkein. "You'll want to make sure you find some Aeci you trust to guard her if you get called away." He glanced back at Hazel. "I don't think our people will harm you, but–"

"It's better safe than sorry." Hazel finished, earning herself a smile from Zodur as he nodded his head in agreement.

"I have a meeting to attend, so you'll have to excuse me, but I will contact Drakkein when we have a proposition for your people," Zodur said as he pushed his hip off the edge of the table.

"We will leave you to your day then," Drakkein said as he turned, flaring out a wing and using it to guide Hazel to the door.

Well, she might not be a skilled negotiator, but she thought that went better than she could have ever expected.

Drakkein kicked his legs up on his couch while he watched Hazel did through his fridge. They'd recently returned to his home after he took her around their city for most of the day. He'd found it fun to show her his world. She'd found it fascinating. Those sky-blue eyes had been stretched wide as she'd eagerly taken in the new world around her.

"I think my first encounter with your father went well, wouldn't you agree?"

"I would." He confirmed.

"I really want our two people to reach some sort of peaceful arrangement. I think it would benefit both colonies." Hazel said, her voice a bit muffled with her head still stuck in his fridge.

"I agree. Our people could learn things from each other." Drakkien's eyes drifted to her ass. Even in the loose clothing he'd given her, he could make out her petite figure, and his cock stirred as he recalled their first time together, and hopefully not their last time.

Mouth stretching wide, Drakkein yawned as he folded a pillow behind his head, so he could relax while keeping an appreciative eye on his human who seemed to have energy to spare.

Hazel's blonde head of hair popped up. "What's this?" She asked, holding up a long white vegetable.

"That's gork. It's a vegetable."

"I figured it was a root vegetable. You have a lot of vegetables and fruits in here." She hitched a thumb over her shoulder at the fridge. "Do you grow these?"

"We do." Drakkein shuffled his wings behind him until he found a comfortable position to lay on them.

"Could you take me to where you grow these?" Her blue eyes turned lighter as excitement sparked through her.

"Tomorrow." Drakkein yawned again. "My wings need a break from all the flying around with you."

Hazel stuck her tongue out at him, and he chuckled as she put the vegetable back into the fridge. He wasn't entirely sure what a tongue out of the mouth meant, but it'd turned her from cute to funny looking.

"If you're looking for something to do, I have some ideas," Drakkein said as he rolled off his couch and approached the kitchen in a lazy stroll. Her butt wiggled in the air as she sorted through his fridge. Oh yeah. He had some ideas of what they could do to pass the time.

Coming up behind her, Drakkein reached out and gripped her waist as he pressed his protruding groin against her butt.

"Oh!" Hazel exclaimed. Then she completely surprised him when she wiggled her butt against his groin. "Oh yeah." Her voice went husky with desire.

"Glad to know I'm not the only one who enjoyed what we did last night."

"It was definitely good." Hazel agreed. "But," she rose and turned in his grasp, "we shouldn't sleep together."

Drakkein's brows drew together. "Why not?" One of his hands stroked up and down her back in a gentle caress.

"I'm here to negotiate peace, and if I had to guess, it goes against ambassador rules to sleep with someone while under talks."

"You're an ambassador?"

"Well… no."

Drakkein shrugged. "Then, there is no problem." His head dipped, and he captured her lips in a possessive kiss. He'd never felt this way towards another woman. Hazel had him dreaming about a possible future. He still wasn't sure whether it was because she was a novelty or because she meant something to him. It was too soon to say she meant something to him, wasn't it?

Hazel resisted his kisses with stiff lips.

"Give in," Drakkein begged her with a light whisper against her lips. "Don't fight the desire between us."

"Where will this go?"

Drakkein shook his head, his lips brushing over hers with the motion. "We can never predict the future, we can only enjoy the present."

At first, Hazel remained tense, but then he felt her relax under his lips.

Drakkein was right, Hazel realized. What was she doing worrying about the future when she could enjoy the present?

His skilled lips slanted over hers once more, and each gentle caress spoke volumes to her. His kisses were hot and possessive, and they left her wondering what he felt towards her.

When his tongue slid between her part lips, she pushed any worries from her mind. Nothing would ruin this.

With each skilled stroke of his tongue against her own, he built the fire burning in her chest. Eagerly, she met his heated kisses with one of her own. Pushing his tongue from her mouth, she entered his. She scraped her tongue against his teeth before quickly retreating back to her mouth.

Drakkein's arms and wings wrapped around her, and she reveled in the warmth that surrounded her. He felt perfect. Like safety and comfort. It was nice, because ever since landing on this planet with the other colonists, she'd felt so uncertain about her future.

This planet was dangerous and unpredictable, and she wasn't about to let a lover like this go without enjoying him to the fullest of her ability.

Hazel's hands stroked up his rock hard chest, enjoying every well-cut ridge. She purred against his lips as his hands explored her in return. His exploring hands dropped to her butt, cupping each orb in a hand. Slowly, he spun them around, and then her eyes widened in surprise as he raised her up and placed her bottom on one of the counters in his kitchen.

Pulling her forward on the counter, Drakkein pulled her legs around his waist, positioning his hard cock against her hot core. Even through their clothing, she could feel his cock pulse with desire, and her body responded with a wave of heat.

Digging her heels into his thighs, Hazel ground her pelvis up against his hard on.

Drakkein hissed against her lips. "That feels good."

"Mmmm hmmm." Hazel agreed as the wicked friction rolled over her clit.

His kisses moved from her lips to her cheek and then down her throat as his hands roamed over her back in gentle strokes until he reached her golden strands of hair. Then his fingers sank deep into her hair, massaging her scalp.

He wasn't the only one exploring, though. Her hands rose to the top of his head. She wanted to feel his horns again. Her fingertips brushed over the rough texture of his horns. There were small ridges around his horns.

Drakkein groaned against her neck as he nipped the skin. "I can feel you playing with my horns."

"You can feel this?" Hazel asked, astonished.

"Our horns have nerves." He placed a hot kiss to her shoulder as he used a finger to pull back her shirt. "If we break them, we feel pain, if you touch them, we can feel it."

"Is it pleasurable?" She asked as she wrapped her hand around one of his black horns and pumped it a couple of times.

Drakkein shrugged as he said, "It feels good, but I wouldn't call it pleasurable."

"Oh, too bad." Hazel pouted her lips before she tugged frantically at his pants. "We need to get these off of you."

"I'm having fun kissing you, though."

Hazel ground her pelvis up against his groin. "I can feel how hard your cock is. You want me." She used her heels to push his groin even closer to her. "You want more than just kisses, you tease."

Leaning forward, Hazel's tongue flicked out from her lips, and she traced the tip of her tongue across his shoulder before kissing his skin.

"Mmm," Drakkein pulled his mouth away from her. "You're right. I want more than just kisses."

Drakkein wasn't sure how much longer he would last. His cock stretched painfully in his pants as Hazel grounded against him like a woman on a mission. The sweet friction felt so good against his engorged length, and he couldn't take it anymore.

Hazel leaned back on the counter, gripped the hem of her shirt with her hands, and ripped the loose material off her body, tossing it into the air.

Knowing she would go for her pants next, Drakkein reached between their bodies and easily undid the two buttons, gripped the waistband and yanked her pants down her legs and let them fall to the floor.

Stepping over the pants, Drakkein undid his pants, and his cock sprang out.

"Oh, yeah." Hazel purred right before she reached out with one of her hands and gripped him. While her hand remained firmly wrapped around his length, her thumb reached out to explore the tip of his cock.

"I love your silvery-grey skin. It's so different than anything I've ever seen."

Drakkein's eyes skimmed over her. She had herself propped up on an elbow, her nipples taut with her desire, and her lust-filled eyes focused on his cock as she explored the length.

"It's beautiful."

Blinking, Drakkein chuckled. "Beautiful?"

"Your cock."

He shook his head. "I'm not sure I would agree with beautiful."

"Fine then." Hazel laughed. "It long and hard, and… unrivaled."

He could agree with that.

"And the tattoos on your horns and arm." Hazel purred the words as her hand left his cock to stroke over the lines of his arm tattoo. "I guess I'm a sucker for a tattooed alien."

Drakkein flexed his arm muscles under her light touch, loving the feel of her hands running over him.

"And then there's your body." Hazel purred. "What I wouldn't give for some chocolate sauce."

"What is this chocolate?" Drakkein asked, not sure why her translator hadn't been able to process the word.

"It's a dessert sauce. Really sweet." She sent him a wink. "And sometimes, we humans, like to drizzle it over our bodies and have our partner lick it off of us."

"I can't find you chocolate, but I am sure I can find something for our next time." Drakkein's heart hitched in his chest, startling and confusing him. Here he was making plans for their future lovemaking, and he wasn't sure how long she would stay.

His mood soured a bit as he realized he might lose her back to her colony until her hand fell back to his cock. She guided the head of his cock to her sweet wet center, where she rubbed it against her clit before positioning at her entrance.

"I need you inside me," Hazel whispered up at him. Her sweet sky-blue eyes were glazed over, a tad darker, like a darkening sky.

She didn't need to beg him. Reaching up, Drakkein took a firm hold of her hips, and with one swift thrust of his hips, he slid his cock deep inside her welcoming warmth.

Hazel let out a hiss of air, and his gaze shot up to her face.

"Did I hurt you?"

"Not hurt." She smiled at him. "Just tight.

You're well endowed."

Drakkein sent her a cocky smile. "Feel free to say that as often and as much as you like."

As he slid his cock out, he pulled back just until the tip was still inside and then thrust back into her, as far her body would take him. The first few thrusts were calm and even, but as he pumped into her and watched her breasts bounce eagerly with the movements, his thrusts grew more erratic and faster.

Drakkein didn't understand it, but this felt right. Hazel felt right like she was meant to be in his arms. Like she and he had been created for each other. He spread his wings wide as he drove into her. He wasn't about to let her go back to her colony without trying to persuade her to stay here with him.

Hazel laid back on the cool counter as she allowed Drakkein to control the momentum of their lovemaking.

A primitive growl of satisfaction filled the air. "So good."

She wanted to agree with him, but she couldn't seem to muster the words. Every stroke of his cock had her body quivering in her desire. Her legs shook as she grew closer to climax.

When she glanced up at Drakkein, she noticed a slight shimmer of sweat to his silvery skin, causing him to glisten in the green lights. "You're incredible." The words were out before she could hold them back.

Drakkein's smile of triumph stole her breath away. His dark eyes held hers as the pleasure rolling through her body shot straight to her brain. Stars of bright light flashed across her vision as her body began to clamp down around his length.

"Drakkein…" She panted. "I'm going to… ah, yes!" Hazel's eyes sank closed as her body shuddered and clamped down on him.

"Hazel." Drakkein ground out as his thrusts slowed and pumped deep into her.

Overwhelming pleasure shot through her, and she was glad Drakkein had taken control because all she wanted was to enjoy the sensations rolling through her. Her eyes opened. She had to see him as they came together.

"So tight." Drakkein groaned right before she felt a searing hotness enter her, and he threw his head back and roared at the ceiling. His dark leathery wings fanned out as he thrust into her, pumping his seed deep inside her.

Hazel moaned in ecstasy as her body coaxed every drop out of him. Their voices mixed and echoed off the walls as a second climax overcame her, and she clawed desperately at the counter underneath her.

How could she ever return to her colony when Drakkein called to her to so deeply? She gazed up at him with love shining bright. Thankfully, his head was still thrown back as he pumped into her, the thrusts becoming lazy as he rode every last wave of pleasure, so he missed her starry-eyed gaze.

Chapter 10

Drakkein loved the feel of his human in his arms. He hugged his arms tighter around her small frame, and he was glad she didn't have wings. Cuddling against a woman when her wings kept hitting him in the face could grow annoying. All he had in front of his face was soft creamy skin, and a thick head of sunlight kissed hair.

Dipping his head, he nuzzled the crevice of her shoulder and neck, breathing in her delicate floral scent. He groaned against her, not in arousal, but in dread. All he wanted to do was remain in the bed with Hazel, but he had things to get to, like speaking with his father to see if a decision had been reached on the humans yet.

All he wanted to do was laze about in bed all day with Hazel, and have more moments like last night.

Hazel mewled in her sleep as she rubbed her butt into his groin, which responded immediately. Even in her sleep, she wanted more of him, and he wished he could give it to her, but then she would thoroughly distract him.

After another couple minutes of cuddling Hazel, Drakkein unwrapped his arms from around her with a sigh and rolled away. Without disturbing her, he pulled back the covers and slipped off the bed, making sure she was still tucked in nice and tight.

Hazel looked so peaceful in her sleep. Her long blonde hair fanned out over the dark pillowcase, and one of her forearms rested between her perfect breasts. He would like nothing better than to always have her in his bed.

Before he could enjoy that, he would have to find peace between their people and a place for her here among his people.

Drakkein fought the urge to jump right back under the covers with her and ignore the day ahead of him.

Ripping his gaze from the beauty in his bed, he pulled on a pair of black pants. He'd put on a shirt, but getting his wings through the holes in the shirts could sometimes be a struggle, so many of their people walked around without the top half of their clothing. It was easier… and faster.

With one last look at Hazel sleeping peacefully on his bed, he strode over to his stone balcony and jumped off the ledge.

"The family wants justice for the death of their son."

Everyone on the Aeci council nodded their horned heads in agreement.

"It is only right that the guilty human or humans are held accountable, especially if they desire peace," Ahre said. As she nodded her head, the dull green lights of the chamber reflected off the gold bands wrapped around her short black horns.

"And how do we get them to turn over these humans?" Moll asked. His silver skin had lost its elasticity of youth and dropped around his jowls. He was one of the oldest council members and usually a bit pessimistic.

"We can send the human woman back with a message of peace and our request of a trial to give our people the justice they deserve." Another council member tossed out.

"We should also send one of our own."

"That is a stupid idea." Moll rolled his eyes.

Ahre's steely eyes pierced the other councilor. "The only person here who isn't thinking is you."

Moll's wings fluttered with his irritation. "How do we choose who goes up there? It could be a death sentence for them."

"It would be dangerous." Ahre mused as she slowly nodded her head and glanced at the table as she thought about Moll's words.

The table went silent as everyone receded into their minds as they thought of a solution.

Drakkein rose from his seat at the table. "I will go."

Drakkein's father glanced up from the other side of the oval table. "We couldn't send you."

"Why not?" Drakkein's brows drew down over his eyes as he scowled at his father and folded his arms in front of his chest.

"You are my only son and will someday take over my position." His father leaned forward and placed his clasped hands on the metal.

"That's true," Moll said with a raised finger.

"One day, you will be a part of this council, and already your mind and ideas have been invaluable."

"If you can't send me, then how can you expect any of our people to volunteer for such a dangerous mission?" Drakkein challenged.

He had his father now. He knew it, and his father knew it. His father was a fair ruler of their people, and he liked to show their people that he would never ask them to do something he wouldn't be comfortable doing.

His father growled with annoyance, one side of his mouth pulling back in an annoyed grimace. "Your mother will never forgive me."

"Mother isn't here to be angry with you." Drakkein sighed. "And if she were here, she'd agree with me." He wasn't sure about that since he didn't remember her, but from the stories his father had told him growing up, he figured it was a pretty decent guess.

"Drakkein is right," Ahre said as she glanced between father and son. "How can we ask anyone else to go up to the alien colony, when we can't even send one of the council?"

His father heaved a sigh as he rubbed his eyes and then ran a silver-skinned hand down his face. "You will go, Drakkein, but," he held up a hand, "we will have several of our people ready to raid the human colony if needed."

"How will you know when to raid?" Drakkein asked with a cocked eyebrow.

His father glanced back at him blankly as he shook his head. "If they send us your body, the humans will have no idea what destroyed them."

Drakkein nodded. "That's fine, as long as you promise to leave Hazel alone."

If the humans were stupid enough to kill him, then they deserved whatever happened, but he couldn't allow Hazel to get caught up in the crossfire. There was no doubt in his mind she was a good and honest person. Perhaps there were more humans in the colony like her, but he wasn't sure he could get his father to promise to keep them alive.

His father's eyes narrowed. "You've grown close to this human fast."

The council shifted in their seats to stare up at Drakkein as they waited for his response. He glanced at each person as he figured out his choice of words.

"I find her fascinating," Drakkein confirmed, but he wasn't sure it was anything more than an infatuation that would slowly dissipate. He enjoyed her company and wanted more time with her, but he also had to be realistic. Their people were so different, and he wasn't even sure how she felt. "I'm not about to join with her if you're worried about that."

"I'm not worried about you joining with the human." His father pierced him with his dark eyes. "Just make sure you don't get too attached. There's no telling if peace talks will work and what arrangement we will form."

"Have you learned anything interesting about the humans?" Moll asked uninterested in Drakkein's love life.

Drakkein shrugged. "From Hazel's reactions, the human colony doesn't seem to be well off. The crops we burned will set them back, I'm sure, and she appeared interested in knowing more about how we grow crops and the water supply we have."

"Nothing about their defenses?" Ivu, another council member, asked.

"Nothing."

"We have more to talk about, then just the colony on the surface. There are concerns about the population outgrowing the space we currently have and putting a strain on our resources." His father began a new topic of discussion as he glanced down at a tablet on the table.

Drakkein sat back down in his seat as his thoughts drifted back to the human woman with sky blue eyes and hair the color of sun-bleached sand. Soon, soon, he would see her again.

Hazel kicked her feet through the air as she waited on Drakkein's bed. She'd woken up to find him gone, his spot on the mattress cold. Once she'd managed to drag herself from the comfortable bed, she pulled on her clothes and scrounged around in his kitchen, and now she sat on his bed watching the city fly by her… literally.

Any Aeci that could fly flew around the city to cut down their travel time. Those who were too young or too old seemed to use the many bridges and stairways that sliced through the underground airway.

Drakkein needed some blinds for his balcony because anyone could fly by and look in, or if they had a good pair of binoculars, they could peer in from the other side of the city. Hazel eyed the opening for the balcony. Hopefully, no one had spied on them last night while they'd been fooling around with each other. What had started in the kitchen had swiftly moved to the bedroom.

"Anyone in there?" Someone knocked on the door while a female voice called out from the other side.

As Hazel popped off the bed and faced the door, it creaked open, and a horned silver-skinned woman's head popped inside the crevice. "Hello?"

"Hello." Hazel waved a hand, and the alien woman walked fully into the room with a smile on her face.

"Drakkein sent me over to show you our hydroponics bay and our aeroponics bay. He said you would find it interesting."

"Where is Drakkein?" Hazel asked, wondering how long until she'd see him again.

"He's caught up in a council meeting." The woman shrugged. "He's not sure when he will get out of it, so he sent a message to me that you might want something more to do than sitting in his room all day." The woman eyed her with a raised brow. "Unless you want to sit in here all day with nothing to do."

"I definitely don't want to wait here all day," Hazel confirmed with a smile. She didn't know the woman, but she seemed trustworthy. It wasn't like she sent off any negative vibes.

"I'm Lul." The woman inclined her head, allowing Hazel a good view of her horned head. Her horns were pretty, with a gold band around one, and both of the tips appeared to have been dipped in gold paint. Then the woman righted herself. "Drakkein failed to tell me your name."

"Hazel." Hazel stepped forward with an outstretched hand.

"What is that for?" Lul asked as she pointed at Hazel's hand.

"Oh, sorry." Hazel withdrew her hand as she shook her head. "It's polite in my world to shake hands when making introductions. I forgot your people don't do that."

Lul's dark eyes widened, but she nodded her head. "Then I am Lul," she reached out a hand, "and you are?"

"Hazel." Hazel repeated as she clasped the woman's hand and firmly shook it. Then they released.

"I am always willing to learn something new about a species." Lul sent her a warm smile. "As you can deduct, we don't get to meet an alien every day, and I'm pleased to have something new and exciting happening around here."

Lul sounded exactly like her. Hazel had lived on this planet for a shorter amount of time, and she was ready for some excitement and fun.

"Should we head out?"

"Lead the way," Hazel said, hoping they would walk rather than fly through the underground city.

"This way." Lul spun on a heel and walked back through the door that led to the living area.

She sighed with relief. There would be no flying involved. She enjoyed flying with Drakkein, a person she, for some reason, trusted. However, she still didn't know Lul all that much, and Hazel didn't need the woman dropping her from a tall height.

A shiver spread through her body as she imagined going splat on the cavern floor.

Jumping into action, Hazel quickly followed after. Lul led her through the living room to another metal door that Hazel had never noticed before. As they stepped through the door, they entered a stone corridor with metal beams for support and structure.

And then her eyes fell on the two male Aeci standing straight as a couple of rods in the corridor. As Lul led the way down the corridor, Hazel didn't miss the two men step up right behind them and begin following.

"Ummm," Hazel cast a nervous glance over her shoulder as she quickened her pace to catch up with Lul, "why are we being followed?"

"Drakkein thought it might be best. As much as we all would like to believe none of our people would exact revenge against you for the death of one of us, there's no way for us to know for sure. Those two," Lul nodded over her shoulder, "are here to protect you."

"I'm not sure whether that makes me feel safer or more in danger." Hazel mused. On one hand, having guards comforted her, but the fact that she needed guards disturbed her a bit.

"Ignore them." Lul waved a hand dismissively.

Hazel figured she really had no choice but to ignore them. It wasn't like she would ask Drakkein to send them away. If he thought they were needed, then they were needed.

They walked through many corridors, most of the corridors were empty except for a few Aeci. It definitely appeared that most of their people preferred to fly when given the chance rather than using the corridors to find their way through the massive underground city. She knew Drakkein had called it a colony, but this was no colony. This was now a thriving city. It was many times bigger than her colony.

After what seemed like an eternity of winding corridors, Lul sent Hazel a smile over her shoulder as they drew up in front of a large metal door. It was a door that was wide enough for a vehicle to drive through.

"Are you ready to see the hydroponics?"

Hazel clapped her hands together in front of her abdomen. "Yes." If her people had a hydroponics system, they might have an easier chance at survival up on the devastating surface. Or maybe aeroponics would be a better fit for them.

Lul blocked a keypad with her body, but Hazel heard the beep of the device as the woman entered a code onto the screen. Then the metal door creaked open as hidden mechanics drew it into the wall.

"Only certain people are allowed in?" Hazel asked, nodding her head to the keypad.

Lul strode through the now open door. "It was determined that access should be limited because, as you know, this planet isn't easy to live on, and we needed to make sure that no accidents happen, intentional or not."

It made sense to Hazel. If someone went nuts and decided to destroy something, they wouldn't want their food source to be disrupted.

"How many people have the code?"

Lul shrugged her shoulders, her shirt bunching up against her neck. "About twenty of us or so. It can be rescinded though," Lul turned and pierced Hazel with her dark eyes. "We do annual psychological evaluations, as well as a few other tests every few months, and there are age limits."

"I assume someone can be too young, but can someone be too old?" Hazel asked as she looked around herself in wonder.

She'd loved her colony's little greenhouse, but this… the Aeci had a forest of a hydroponics bay. The ceiling high above, beamed with large lights to help the plants grow. Massive white tubs formed many rows, and they went on for as far as her eye could see, and each section grew different plants if she knew anything about foliage.

The trickle of water entered her ears, and as she peered over the edge of a tub, she saw some alien fish swimming around in the water. The orange fish had zig-zagging lines of yellow across their sides, and they appeared to have spikes on their dorsal fins.

"Someone can be too old as well," Lul confirmed as she walked up beside Hazel. "These are tlurip. They are very tasty, and we have a section of our city just for farming them."

"Do these systems waste a lot of water?" Hazel asked as they walked deeper into the hydroponics bay.

Lul shook her black hair. "We've got several systems in place to make sure we don't lose too much water. We don't want to waste anything we don't have too, and we have fail safes in place to make sure that any leaks don't leak more than we would want them to in an emergency." She fluttered her leathery wings.

"This is impressive."

After a few minutes of walking around, Lul plucked an orange oblong fruit off a branch and held it out to Hazel.

Hazel took the fruit and studied it between her hands.

"Take a bite." Lul waved a silver-skinned hand in Hazel's direction. "The flesh is edible as well."

Sucking in a breath, Hazel decided to trust the other woman. She couldn't believe Drakkein would send someone to show her around that he didn't trust with her safety. It wasn't like he loved her, but she did believe he wanted peace between their peoples as much as she did.

Raising the fruit to her mouth with both of her hands, she opened her mouth wide and bit into the flesh of the fruit. Sourness hit her tongue, puckering her face before a wave of sweetness pushed the sour off her taste buds.

"Woah!" Hazel's eyes widened as she pulled the fruit away to see blue flesh staring back at her. "It's blue inside? I don't think I've seen anything like it."

"Probably not. It's native to our home planet, and a delicacy. That one bite you had would have been about five hundred thousand credits."

"Wooooow." Hazel drew out the word. "That's a lot of money."

"Don't worry, we won't charge you." Lul winked at her with a flutter of her wings as she chuckled.

"Good." Hazel laughed, a bit uneasily. "I don't think I could afford it."

"It's not as expensive here as back on our homeworld, or no one would be able to afford it in a colony. No one here is massively rich."

"That's good to hear. I'd hate to rack up a huge bill." Hazel took another bite, finishing off the small fruit. Her eyes pinched tight as her mouth puckered, and then the muscles in her face relaxed as sweetness washed over her tongue. "I'm guessing your people wouldn't be willing to share this technology with my people?" She hedged.

The smile disappeared off Lul's face. "I wouldn't be the person to say. The decision to share our hydroponic and aeroponic supplies with your people would have to be made by the council."

Too bad. It had been worth an ask, though. She supposed she would just need to have another meeting with Drakkein's father.

"Should we head to the aeroponics bay?" Lul asked.

"Show the way." Hazel waved a hand in the air. She was eager to see more. Even if the Aeci wouldn't share their technology, Hazel could at least walk away with knowledge from what she'd seen and hope her people had the supplies to replicate it.

Chapter 11

"Duck!"

Hazel hit the metal floor as a plasma shot seared past her head, causing the air to sizzle next to her ear. Glancing up from where she crouched against the floor, she watched Lul tackled a male Aeci to the metal floor of the corridor. A man who held a plasma rifle. A couple shots seared into the ceiling as they grappled for possession of the gun.

Glancing over her shoulder, Hazel caught sight of the two guards in a hand to hand fight with two other Aeci. Their wings were held tight to their backs, probably to prevent their opponents from injuring them during the fight.

"Grab the woman!" One of the opposing Aeci yelled at his companions.

Boots thumped against the metal floor, and when Hazel figured out which direction it came from, she spotted an Aeci bearing down on her. His dark eyes pierced her as a growl curled one side of his silver lips. Jumping to her feet, she balled up her fists and threw a leg behind her to brace herself.

It wasn't like Hazel knew how to defend herself, but she wasn't the type of person to go down without a fight.

A smirk lifted one side of the Aeci's mouth as he bared down on her. His wings spread wide, cutting off her view of Lul. She hoped the other woman didn't get injured, but in the meantime, she had to protect herself.

"You will pay for the sins of your people." The Aeci growled through a clenched jaw as he swung a fist at her, clearly wanting a fist fight rather than shoot her dead in one shot. He wanted this to last longer. To torture her.

Damn.

Hazel kind of wished he would finish her off quickly rather than beat her to a pulp. She hoped she could use her small size to her advantage and dodge him long enough for someone to come to her aid.

Ducking down, Hazel barely avoided getting punched in the side of the face, but as she was busy dodging his fist, she didn't notice his leg sweep out. His foot slammed into her calf, knocking her to the ground. As she struggled on the floor like a beached fish, his leg pulled back, and when she noticed his foot coming straight for her side, she curled up and wrapped her hands around her neck.

The force of his kick knocked the breath out of her lungs, but when he pulled back again, she groaned in pain as she darted back onto her feet and threw a wild punch. Desperate to hit anything.

Chuckling, the Aeci slammed a closed fist into the side of her cheek. Blood filled her mouth as her teeth sliced the inside of her cheek. The metal floor rushed up to smack her in the face as black dots filled her vision. As the darkness claimed her, she could have sworn she heard a roar of anger echo down the corridor, but she didn't see from who it came from as the darkness swamped her.

Drakkein scarcely believed what his eyes told him. After the council meeting let out, he'd been eager to meet up with Lul and Hazel on their tour. He wished he could have shown Hazel the hydroponics himself, but the meeting had gone longer than he'd thought it would.

After he'd found the hydroponics bay empty, he'd headed down the corridor for the aeroponics. Then the sounds of a fight had reached his ears. When he rounded a corner, he'd faltered. Lul and the guards fended off Aeci.

Searching the crowd, he watched Hazel fall to the ground, a trickle of red blood leaving her small mouth.

A roar of rage ripped up his throat as he shot forward like a rocket. Striding past the guards who fought off some of the attackers, Drakkein burst into a run, slamming into the Aeci who dared touch Hazel before the man could kick her again. The force of his weight knocked the other man off his feet.

As they landed on the metal floor, Drakkein held the sharp tip of his wing to the man's throat. "What are you doing?" He snarled down at the man. He pressed the tip deeper into the man's throat, causing a bead of blood to trickle out.

"She killed my brother."

Drakkein saw red, but he restrained himself from pressing his claw any deeper or beating the man senseless. "She had nothing to do with your brother's death." He had no way of proving it, but he couldn't see Hazel being a party to anything so horrible. "Her people are responsible, yes, but not her."

"I want justice." The man ground out as he pushed himself onto an elbow, and Drakkein backed his claw off as the man moved. He might want to kill the man for harming Hazel, but he didn't need the trouble of a death on his hands.

"Killing her won't bring justice, just more bloodshed." Drakkein calmed as he realized the situation was cooling down. The man couldn't even look up at Drakkein, and he took it as a sign that the man was ready to give up. "The council discussed how best to go about getting your justice. Give us time before you do anything rash."

"I didn't know." The man grumbled, still unable to meet Drakkein's eye.

"Here," Drakkein held out a hand as he stood.

The man finally lifted his gaze. He stared at Drakkein's offered hand for a long second before accepting the assistance.

"What you have done here will need its own justice," Drakkein stated simply. "Now leave and remain in your home until someone comes to get you."

"That's enough!" The man barked at the Aeci who'd joined him in the attack.

Drakkein glanced around to see the fighting finally break up. "The same goes for all of you who fought here today. Go home, and do not venture out until told you may." He pointed at the two guards who finally had enough space to draw their plasma pistols, "Make sure all of them get to their homes."

The guards nodded their heads as they

gathered up the attackers and slowly guided them down the corridor at gun point.

"How is she?" Lul rushed up to his side breathing hard, her bottom lip split from where she'd been punched.

Drakkein spun on a booted heel and bent down next to Hazel, who still laid on the floor. Pulling a device out of his belt, he held it over her, so it could scan. A sigh of relief left his lungs when the device reported back that her heartbeat, and she breathed. "She is alive, but we should get her back to the hospital to make sure she isn't seriously harmed." The device was for his people, not hers, and he wanted to make sure nothing happened to her.

"I can take her if you want."

"No," Drakkein gently scooped Hazel into his arms. "Find my father and tell him I want to leave the moment Hazel is ready for travel. The sooner we find peace between our people, the better. Tensions will only rise on our end as we wait for a trail."

Lul nodded sharply before turning and sprinting in the opposite direction Drakkein headed.

"You're a bit of trouble," Drakkien remarked to the unconscious woman in his arms. "First, you set out on your own to a people you don't know to seek peace, and then you happen to cross paths with the deceased's brother." Although, Drakkein was sure this was coincidence. The brother must have sought her out on purpose after hearing there was a human in their city.

Picking up his pace, Drakkein raced toward the closest balcony. When it came into sight, he stretched his wings wide, and the moment he broke free from the corridor, his wings beat a strong rhythm, lifting them off the ground. Then they soared through the air as he rushed her back to the hospital, hoping her injuries weren't life-threatening.

Chapter 12

Wind whipping past her face, woke Hazel as her aching head tried to catch up with recent events. She could scarcely believe they'd been attacked in the corridor. The men had materialized all around them like silver-skinned demons.

Glancing around, she found herself cradled in a pair of strong arms, and when she looked up, she spotted Drakkein's grim lined face above her. Past his head, she watched his massive black leathery wings beat a powerful rhythm through the air.

"Where are we going?"

"You're awake." His dark eyes glanced down, and the tightness in his jaw relaxed a bit. "That's good." His dark eyes softened. "How do you feel? Does anything hurt?"

"My jaw," Hazel said as she raised a hand to rub the side of her face where she'd been punched. "It's tender, but I don't think anything is broken." And she was relieved to realize none of her teeth had been knocked loose. She placed a hand to her ribcage, and although she'd been kicked, it didn't feel like any bones were broken. All in all, she'd escaped fairly unscathed. "Where are we going?"

"To the hospital. I want you to get checked out."

It sounded good to her, so she wasn't about to protest. Better safe than sorry. Settling back in his arms, she let his body heat warm her as the cool underground air tried to cause her a chill.

With a snap, his wings pulled up, slowing them down before he landed, jostling her a bit. "Sorry," he apologized.

"I'm fine." Hazel quickly reassured him.

Drakkein squeezed her lightly as he walked towards the hospital doors, and her heart flipped in happiness. She didn't want to worry him, but his concern did warm her and spoke volumes to her about his feelings toward her. Then again, maybe he was simply worried about her dying, and any potential peace dying with her. No. She didn't believe that. It was most likely a mix of the two.

Drakkein strode through the entrance, barely allowing the clear glass doors to part for him, causing Hazel to close her eyes in fear that they would just bust through the glass. Once they entered, she let out the breath she'd been holding.

"How can I help you?" A woman from behind the desk looked up, no concern lighting up her dark eyes.

"A fight broke out, and she was injured. I want her checked out." Drakkein strode straight past the desk.

"Wait!" The woman barked as she jumped up from her seat. "I haven't told you where to go with her."

"Any empty room will do," Drakkein remarked over his shoulder.

The woman grumbled something under her breath about Drakkein being a stubborn and imperious man. Peeking around his silver-skinned arm, Hazel caught sight of the woman trailing behind them. Her wings fluttered in irritation behind her as she rubbed a hand over one of her black and gold horns.

"Maybe you should be a bit nicer." Hazel turned her eyes back up to Drakkein. "The woman is just trying to do her job, and it isn't like I'm going to die in the next couple of minutes."

"We need you to be checked out, and I don't want to wait."

"Well, just make sure you apologize." Hazel insisted.

"Here," Drakkein stepped into a room and set her down on a medical bed. "Lay down." He pressed a hand to her chest, and Hazel sank back against the soft pillow. Then he turned to the woman who'd followed them, "Get a doctor. I want her examined."

The woman mumbled some intelligible words as she marched out of the room, her spine as stiff as a rod, and her wings pressed tightly against her back in irritation of being bossed around.

"You really should be a little nicer with your words."

Drakkein glanced down at her but didn't respond. Instead, he clutched one of her hands in one of his. "As we wait for the doctor to show," he turned his head to glance down at her, "I have something to discuss with you from the council meeting today."

"Yeah?" Hazel cocked her head to the side and winced when her jaw protested the movement.

"The council has decided to seek peace with your people, and to do that, they will send someone up to the surface to meet with your people."

"Hmmm." Hazel murmured as she took in the information.

"What do you think of the idea?"

Hazel glanced down to her free hand, where she picked at the thin blanket underneath her. "I think it sounds dangerous for whoever they chose to send up. I can't promise how my people will react." She glanced up, meeting his dark eyes. He had more to tell her, she was sure of that. "Is there anything else you need to pass along?"

"They've already chosen who will be sent up with you to discuss peace."

Her eyes narrowed on him as she got the feeling she wouldn't enjoy the answer. "Who?"

"Me."

Hazel's hand clenched around his until her fingers went white. "No."

Drakkein's silvery lips curved up in a smile. "Yes. I will be sent up with you."

"Then I won't go back," Hazel said with a definitive nod of her head.

"Either way, I will be sent up, with or without you," Drakkein said. "The decision was already made. We will attempt peace with your people, or we will destroy the threat."

"Destroy… the threat?" Hazel's heart fluttered in her chest at the idea that his people would stage a full-on attack.

He squeezed her hand back. "It would only be as a last resort, but you have to see it from our point of view. Your people landed on our planet and made a home here, and we were willing to let you remain up there, and then you killed one of our men while he was on the surface hunting. If your people can't promise some sort of peace, it means our hunting parties will have more to fear than just large reptiles killing them."

As much as Hazel wanted to protest, to shake her head and scream at him that she didn't understand, she did. The sad truth was that she did understand. And her people had been the first to make the wrong move.

"I worry what my people could do to you." Hazel's voice cracked at the end.

Drakkein squeezed her hand again. "I will be fine."

"When do we head up to the surface?" She asked, hoping it would be in a few days… or maybe a couple of months or years.

"The moment the doctor clears you, we will head up."

Hazel nodded her head as she hoped the doctor would find some reason to hospitalize her for the rest of her life.

Damn that doctor. He'd strode into the room, healed a few cuts and abrasions on Hazel's face and abdomen with a small device, and then declared her well enough to leave the hospital.

Hazel smacked a hand against Drakkein's bed as thoughts churned through her mind. All she wanted to do was come up with a plan that didn't involve Drakkein coming with her.

"What did my bed do to you?" Drakkein chuckled from behind her.

Spinning on the sheet, Hazel glared at him. "I'm upset with your doctor, not your bed."

Drakkein chuckled some more. "And why is that?"

"He insisted I was well enough to travel up to the surface." She smacked the bed again. "I don't want you coming up to the surface. I don't think any Aeci should join me to the surface. There's no guarantee they will ever come back alive."

"Mmm." Drakkein stepped towards her, laid his large warm hands on her shoulders, and gently guided her back on his bed as his body followed her down. His lips landed across hers. "Let's worry about it later, after we enjoy some time together."

"But–"

Drakkein deepened his kiss, preventing her from voicing anymore of her concerns over him joining her. It was an unfair tactic on his part. When he continued his onslaught, Hazel's eyes sank closed as she enjoyed the weight of his body pressing her into the soft mattress.

His hands skimmed up her sides to her shoulders, and then he trailed kisses from her lips down to her neck. "Let's get these clothes off of you." He murmured between each kiss.

"Okay."

A loud rip filled her ears, and Hazel jerked up, only to glance down and found her shirt ripped from her neckline down to the hem. "What the?"

"Whoops." Drakkein leaned back and eyed his handy work with a twinkle in his dark eyes. "I guess I was too eager to see you naked and sprawled out in front of me."

"You ruined a perfectly fine shirt." Hazel frowned at him. Everything in her colony was precious. People did whatever they could to make sure their clothing stayed clean and unripped because there was no telling when the next shirt or pair of pants might come along.

Drakkein shrugged above her as he pushed her breasts together with his palms. "We will recycle it, and I have another I can give you."

Hazel rolled her eyes. "Don't tell me you're one of those guys."

"Which guys?" He asked as he lowered his face and nuzzled one side of a plump breast.

"The kind who would prefer me naked and wet all day every day."

Drakkein paused in his fondling of her breasts. "Is that a possibility?"

Her mouth gaped open until she spotted the teasing glint in those deep eyes. "Oh! You!" She playfully smacked a hand against his head, making sure to miss his horns.

Drakkein chuckled against her skin before sucking a tight bud into his mouth. His tongue lapped against her like this was his last chance to enjoy her body, and she feared it might be their last time together. Soon they would be sucked right back into the conflict she'd come here to resolve, and there was no telling what the future would hold for them.

Laying back down against the mattress, Hazel let the pleasure wash over her. Her hands greedily sank into Drakkein's soft mane of black hair. When her hands bumped into his horns, she wrapped them around the rough curved lengths, and slowly pushed them, guiding his head down her body.

Drakkein seemed more than happy to oblige her. He trailed kisses down her abdomen until he reached her pants. "We will have to take these off."

"Try not to rip them off." Hazel breathed on a heated sigh.

"I'll do my best." He placed one more kiss against the fluttering skin of her abdomen before pulling back, undoing the buttons on her pants, and then commanded her, "Lift your butt." When she did, he slipped the pants from her body and discarded them with a flick of his hand. "Now, spread your thighs."

Hazel did as he commanded, the cool air of the room rushing up to brush every delectably hot part of her.

Drakkein stared down at her for what felt like an eternity. She was gorgeous. Spread for his pleasure, her knees slightly bent. His gaze raked over the woman in front of him. Her wet engorged folds called his name, but he stilled himself and took her in. For all he knew, this would be the last time they had to enjoy together. He didn't want to admit it to Hazel, but he did worry for his safety when they left for her colony.

Life was always unpredictable, which was the very same reason why he planned to enjoy himself and make sure she enjoyed herself.

"Absolutely beautiful."

A light pink spread across her cheeks at his compliment, and although his people didn't blush, he knew it was something she did when she felt embarrassed or flattered.

"Done looking? Because I know of some things that require your attention." Hazel wiggled her body, causing her breasts to sway.

Chuckling, Drakkein dropped to his knees beside the bed, wrapped his hands around her waist, and drew her across the mattress, closer to his face. "Exquisite." He whispered before he leaned in and lapped at her.

Hazel moaned deliriously. He glanced up as he tongued her to see blatant desire burning in her blue eyes. As his gaze drifted over her, his eyes lingered on the pert pink nipples. The perky nipples called his name, begging him to show them some attention.

Stroking his hands up her waist, he cupped each full breast. The soft flesh molded to his hands. It was so supple, and if his face wasn't already occupied, he would be more than happy to nuzzle them again.

Hazel's hands reached down and grabbed a forceful hold of his horns. Then she applied pressure, pushing his face further down, and then guiding him back up. Drakkein was more than willing to allow her to use him to bring her pleasure.

"Oh… Drakkein." Hazel sighed as her hips bucked under his face.

His cock pulsed in his pants at the need in her voice. He wanted nothing more than to plunge his cock deep inside her, but he also loved having her come around his face.

Hazel's body began to vibrate around him as her thighs clamped down around his face, her hips bucking wildly, riding his tongue with abandon.

"Oh! Oh!" Hazel's head thrashed across his sheets as she came around his face. "Feels soooo good!" She nearly screamed at the ceiling of his bedroom.

Drakkein pinched her nipples between his fingers, and he felt her shatter.

"Yes!" Hazel screamed, her head and torso coming off his mattress. After a few seconds, she collapsed back onto his bed. "Oh… yes." Her thighs relaxed, falling off to the sides.

Drakkein lapped at her one last time before rising back onto his feet, quickly shedding his pants, his cock eagerly springing free.

A gasp of delight drew his attention back to the bed, where Hazel had propped herself onto her elbows. Her delicate pink tongue darted out, wetting her lips as she gazed hungrily at his cock.

"Do you want me inside you?" He asked.

"I do."

"I want to hear you say the words."

Her sky-blue eyes glanced up at him. "I want you inside me, Drakkein."

It was all he needed to hear. In a couple of strides, he stood beside the bed. "Scoot further up the bed." He commanded her.

Hazel quickly scurried back up the bed before resting her head on one of the fluffy pillows adorning his bed. "Come and get me." She wiggled her eyebrows at him.

With a smirk curving one side of his mouth, Drakkein quickly joined her on the bed. Carefully, he folded his leathery wings tightly behind his back so they wouldn't get in the way. Laying next to her, he trailed a hand down to the juncture of her thighs. His fingers deftly slid against her slick lips.

"So wet." He groaned.

"Yes." Hazel agreed as her hand found his cock, stroking him as he slid his fingers deep inside her.

Drakkein shuddered, and Hazel moaned.

"Oh my goodness," Hazel's hips bucked.

"Needy." He chuckled.

"I don't know what it is about you." Hazel shook her head. "All I want to do is spend the rest of my life with you in this bed. As crazy as it sounds."

Drakkein pumped his fingers in and out of her, adding a second to the first. "I know what you mean." His chest felt like it might explode with all the emotions he felt. They were all a jumble inside him, but he recognized a few. There was curiosity to know her better, and desire, lots and lots of desire, as well as something that felt strangely like love. There were also more serious emotions like respect for her loyalty to her people, and pride in her persistence. He could imagine having her by his side for life. He was positive there wouldn't be a dull moment with her.

"Oh, yes!" Hazel's cries of pleasure drew him back to the gorgeous woman in his arms. "I need you inside me."

"I'm having fun playing with you."

Hazel's hand abandoned his cock to seize his hand. "Now."

"Then you'll ride me," Drakkein said as he rolled onto his back, his cock standing rod straight in the air.

"Eagerly." Hazel smiled as she flipped over and straddled him in one fluid movement.

Gripping his cock in one hand, he held it steady as Hazel lowered herself onto him.

Drakkein clenched his jaw as she slowly eased onto him. "Your body is so wet and ready for me."

"Mmm hmmm," She agreed as she sank further down his shaft.

Her wet engorged folds hugged him in their tight clutches, and he wasn't sure he wouldn't just come right then and there. His hands cupped her breasts, massaging the soft flesh as she sank to the hilt. Then she used her legs to pump him in easy even strokes.

Tilting forward, she braced her hands on his chest, her fingernails lightly digging into his flesh, but he didn't mind. The pain was a bit pleasurable.

Hazel increased the pace. "Oh yes… oh yes." She moaned as she flipped her golden locks over one shoulder, the strands tickling his bare skin.

Soon she gasped his name in between her moans as she took every inch of his length.

"Forgive me, but I want a faster pace," Drakkein said as his hands came down to wrap around her waist.

"Good," Hazel panted, "because my leg muscles are growing tired."

It was all he needed to hear. Using his grip on her waist, he increased the rhythm until he had her breasts bouncing wildly above him. The dusky tips seemed to tease him, their tight buds just begging to be sucked.

Hazel rose her hands to her breasts, cupping them and pinching her nipples.

"Stars woman. You are perfect." Drakkein groaned as the pressure grew in his cock. "You tempt me beyond reason."

His thrusts changed, becoming more frantic and uneven. Her body trembled around him, shuddering in her ecstasy as her tight sheath began to clamp down around him. Hazel's back arched, throwing her hands behind her back to land on his thighs.

"I can't hold… on… any longer." Drakkein grunted.

"Yes. Come inside me."

Drakkein's eyes closed as he came into her tight sheath. Her inner walls pulsed around his length, coaxing every last drop out of him.

Hazel slumped over his chest as their climaxes finished. His cock twitched inside her, enjoying the feel of her wrapped around him.

With a content sigh, Drakkein ran his hands over the smooth skin of her back, down to her shapely buttocks, which he cupped as he placed kisses into the crevice of her neck and shoulder. "We should get some rest before we head up, so we have a clear mind."

"Sounds good to me," Hazel said, sounding like she'd already fallen asleep on his chest.

Twisting over on the bed, he withdrew from inside her and tucked her firmly into his chest. If her people ended up killing him, at least he would die a happy man.

Chapter 13

Despite everything Drakkein had told Hazel, his stomach was in knots. The humans would have him in the palm of their hands. They could either start the journey to peace and healing or kill him and start a war that would end in a few of his people dying and the human colony being annihilated.

He slid his helmet over his head. It made his head look bulbous to accommodate his horns.

"Why did you guys pick a desert planet again?" Hazel asked.

Turning, he found her watching him as she wrapped some fabric around her head and neck to protect her skin from the harsh rays of the sun. Even her people couldn't stand the sun.

"We figured no one else would choose to colonize the planet. We were wrong."

Hazel let out a bark of laughter as she clutched her stomach. "It was the very same reason we chose this planet. We figured no one had, and no one would want the planet from us. It could be our haven from the complications of space."

"It seems desert planets are more popular than anyone would have believed."

"I guess." Hazel chuckled as she shook her head. Her blue eyes twinkling with her amusement. "The rest of the universe would think us all insane for fighting over such a hot and dangerous planet."

Drakkein typed a few commands into the screen on his wrist to run a quick systems check on his suit, and when everything came back in the green, he asked, "Ready to head up to the surface?"

"No," Hazel heaved a sigh, "but I don't think I really have a choice in the matter, do I?"

"I'm going up whether you join me or not, but," he rested an armored hand on her shoulder, "if you go with me, I will at least have one voice on my side. A better chance at not being shot on sight."

"True." She sent him a wink. "You can always expect me to be on your side." She sent him a thumbs up, which he found adorable. It wasn't a gesture his people made, but he liked it.

Drakkein sent her a thumbs up, finding the gesture strange. "Let's get up there then." He took the lead as he guided her down a long corridor lit with green lights.

"Why all the green lights around the city?"

"It's easier on our eyes and skin. Our home planet is bathed in green light and much cooler than this planet."

They fell back into silence as they pulled up in front of a thick metal door. Holding up his wrist to the door, it read the chip and slowly eased open.

Bright sunlight streamed through the open door, and if his suit hadn't been covering his skin, it would have been seared immediately. "Come on." He reached out and grabbed a hold of her hand and tugged her along behind them. As they walked into the sandy desert environment, he heard the door hiss closed behind them.

"I'm nervous."

Drakkein squeezed her hand, hoping to give her some modicum of confidence. "You said some of your people would rather have peace than fight. We have to believe those voices will be powerful enough to overcome anyone who wants a fight."

"Still, there are people who would rather try and take you guys on." Hazel sighed heavily beside him as she trudged over the grains of sand, which tried to gobble up their feet as they walked across it. "We have a lot of hot-headed young men and some old hot-headed men in the colony."

"I don't want to cause you any pain, if and when your people harm me, but my father had to choose someone." Drakkein glanced to his side to see her sky blue eyes swirling with her mixture of emotions. He wished he could alleviate her fears, but he couldn't promise everything would be alright. So, he just squeezed her hand again.

As they walked around a large sand dune, the human colony came into sight. The silver metal walls beamed the sun in every direction like a beacon to anything and everything in the desert. He was slightly surprised they hadn't been attacked by some of the local wildlife. The large desert reptiles wouldn't have too hard a time scaling those short walls.

Hazel stopped in her tracks and tugged him back. "We shouldn't go."

Turning, Drakkein raised his gloved hands to her shoulders, and he rubbed them gently, easing some of the tension in her body out. "We have to do this for our people. If a war starts between us, it won't only be your people who are harmed, but mine. We have to believe that your people will see reason."

"I hear and understand the words coming out of your mouth, but I also know how humans can be. We have such a great ability to love and embrace new ideas, but we also have a great way of making a mess of things."

"We've gone over this, Hazel. There is no choice. We need to continue with the plan." He couldn't simply turn around and head back to his people without a promise of peace talks.

Hazel's blue eyes glistened with unshed tears, and his heart shattered in his chest. "Don't cry."

"I can't promise I won't cry when and if my people do something cruel to you." She sucked in an unsteady breath before letting it out in a rush.

"I need you to hold it together for me. You need to be my voice if anything happens." He stroked a gloved thumb over the fabric covering her cheek. "I need you to be thinking rationally."

She nodded her head. She didn't utter another word, but he took her nod as acceptance and permission to continue their mission.

Grabbing a hold of her hand once more, Drakkein led the way across the sand.

A cry went up, as men on the curtain wall of the colony spotted them approaching. Hazel just hoped they wouldn't start shooting before they had a chance to see it was her. More men ran up to the curtain wall, and one of them looked like her father. He stood tall among the other men, and there was his distinctive puffed out chest that she loved.

Relief swam through her at the sight of him. Her father wouldn't let the colonists shoot them down, not until he knew why she brought an alien to them.

"I think you should stand behind me."

"Why?" Drakkein's voice came through the speakers on his helmet.

"So, they can't shoot you as easily." As much as Hazel trusted her father, she still wanted to be careful.

"If any of them are decent shots, then I don't think you will provide much protection." Drakkein chuckled. "You're a bit smaller and shorter than me. One good sniper and I'd be blown away."

Hazel was positive he would have winked at her if he didn't have a helmet covering his face. She rolled her eyes. "Fine. Don't. I just figured it would help keep you safer."

"If it makes you feel better," Drakkein said as he dropped back a couple paces and began walking behind her.

"Thanks," Hazel said over her shoulder without her gaze leaving the compound in front of her. Then she drew up as she stared at the men and women on the wall. Raising her hands, she drew back the cloth protecting her head and neck from the sun.

"Hazel?!" Her father's angry voice carried down to her. "What in blazes do you think you're doing down there?"

"Someone needed to seek peace with the aliens." She tossed back, but without any anger. She didn't need to get into a yelling match with her father and raise tensions right before introducing Drakkein.

"And you brought one of them here?" Her father's blue eyes widened in disbelief. "Do you know what they did while you were gone?" He motioned wildly with a hand.

Hazel shook her head.

"They burned the rest of our crops."

She kept her face straight, despite her shock. But they hadn't worked out peace yet with the Aeci, so it wasn't like they'd betrayed her trust.

"That's why I brought him." Hazel held a hand out to indicate Drakkein. "He is here to talk peace with you. Their people would rather find a peaceful way to coexist than have an ongoing war."

Her father just stared down at her, and she found it hard to read his reaction. What was he thinking? Then he turned and huddled up with the rest of the council on the curtain wall.

"This doesn't appear to be going well so far," Drakkein whispered from behind her.

"There's a reason I asked you not to come." She hissed back. She didn't mean to be snippy with him, but she worried for his safety. It was the first time in her life that she understood the saying about having a heart outside of her chest. All she wanted to do was bundle him up and shove him inside her chest, so she could keep him safe from her people.

Then her father faced them again. "You may come in, but we will shoot him if he makes a wrong move."

Every man on the wall leveled their plasma weapons at them.

A tremor of fear rocked through Hazel as the metal doors opened, and a trickle of sweat dripped between her shoulder blades. There would be no turning around now, she supposed.

"Start walking," Drakkein whispered from behind her. "Before they lose patience with us."

Straightening her back, Hazel strode forward with Drakkein hot on her heels. The moment they crossed through the doors, they snapped closed behind them. They were now trapped inside. Never before had the colony felt like home, but neither had it felt like a prison. With Drakkein's life hanging in the balance though, it caused her heart rate to speed with fear.

Men surrounded them immediately, separating her and Drakkein in a matter of seconds.

When the men guided him away from her, she attempted to follow, but Theo stepped into her path.

"How are you holding up?" Theo asked, his grey eyes skimming over her like he was looking for any injuries. She supposed it made sense since he currently studied under the colony's doctor.

"I'm fine." Hazel raised herself on her toes and peered over Theo's shoulders as she tried to spot Drakkein. "Where are they taking him?"

"To a holding cell." Her father's voice said from behind her.

"Why?" She spun around. "He wants to talk about peace between our people."

"As leader, I have to make sure about that." Her father reached out a hand and clamped it down on her shoulder. "I'm willing to talk peace but we need to make sure of his intentions before we begin any talks."

"You aren't going to torture him, are you?" Hazel wrung her hands in front of her abdomen.

"It almost sounds like you care for this alien." Theo accused. His eyes narrowed on her, and his lips pulled back in a frown.

"Maybe I do." Hazel shot back, tired of his attentions. He had no right to play the jealous boyfriend.

Theo's grey eyes turned frosty despite the sweltering heat of the day, but she refused to flinch away. She was done with him and his attitude. He might be good looking and a doctor, but it didn't mean every woman would fall at his feet, shaking with desire.

"I got to know Drakkein and his people." She glanced back at her father. "They might look different than us, but they came here for the very same reasons, to escape persecution and carve out a place to live their lives in peace."

"Here," her father raised a hand and guided her to some shade, "let's get inside, so we don't have any eavesdroppers."

Hazel glanced around and found nearly everyone in the colony gathered around. Their eyes were wide and full of concern, interest, and hope for a little bit of gossip. It wasn't like there were a lot of thrilling things happening in this colony unless you counted the aliens burning the crops. As much as they desired less drama from Earth, they couldn't resist listening in.

"Okay," Hazel said as she allowed her father to guide her towards the cafeteria, which would be empty at this time of day.

When Theo tried to follow them inside, her father instructed him, "Guard the door."

"I can guard it from the inside." Theo walked into the cafeteria and folded his arms in front of his chest.

Her father rubbed the back of his neck with a hand but relinquished. "Fine. Just make sure no one comes in here." Then he directed her to a seat as he took one. "Why did you leave, Hazel?" His blue eyes filled with concern.

"No one here seemed to be taking this seriously. We need peace, dad." Hazel pleaded with him. "You should see their home."

"What was it like?" Her father's blue eyes danced with interest.

"They have an underground city, and just like us, they are colonists. They've only been here for a couple of generations. You just have to see their city to believe it." Hazel shook her head as she searched for words. "They used their ships to build the city, but when their people began to outgrow what they had, they used the rock of the planet to build even more."

"Sounds like a place that needs to be seen to be understood."

"It is." Hazel relaxed a bit as she realized her father really was interested. "The aliens use their wings as their main mode of transportation around their city."

"Did they fly you around?"

"Drakkein did, and to say it was exhilarating would be understatement," Hazel noticed the tension easing from her father's shoulders.

"They never harmed you?"

"Well," Hazel grimaced.

"They hurt you?" His blue eyes flashed steely grey as his hands balled into fists.

"What would you expect from aliens?" Theo commented with a snobbish air.

Hazel sent him a glare before turning back to her father. "They saved me when I passed out in the desert. As I stayed there, I explored the city, and, well, the brother of the alien we killed punched me, but," she waved a hand, "I'm fine."

"Hmm." Her father said as he leaned back. "Why save you when they burned our crops? It seems like they are sending mixed messages to me. Either they want us dead, or they don't."

Hazel found it hard to disagree with her father.

"Just like us, they have some people who want peace and some people who want justice, and they're willing to do whatever it takes to get it." Hazel glanced over at Theo, who still stood by the door, watching and listening to the conversation. "We started this when we killed one of their men. It's our fault."

"A man who would have killed us," Theo commented, and she sent him a glare.

"We only have your word and the word of the other men with you."

"You only have the word of some aliens that say it was anything but self-defense."

"You say that, but it isn't for you or me to decide. We should hold a trial and see what comes of it."

"A trial filled with aliens?" Theo snorted. "They would see us dead."

"I'm sure we could fill the trial with your peers." Hazel glanced over at her father. "They want justice for the death, and I think that just means they want a trial. They want to know what happened and why our people would have killed one of their own. If it was a justified death, then they'll accept it, but they need this."

Her father nodded his head. "I will have to talk with the council, and it might come down to a vote amongst the colonists."

Sucking a breath, Hazel added, "I don't know if this will help you make your decision or not, but if they can't find justice, it might start a war." She held up a hand when her father opened his mouth. "They aren't threatening us–"

"It sounds like a threat to me," Theo commented, earning a glare from her father.

"It's a warning, and one we should heed because we don't want to get into a war with the Aeci." Hazel rubbed a hand across her arm. "They might be colonists like us, but they have a huge underground city with hundreds of them, maybe more." It wasn't like she'd been given a full tour of the city.

Her father nodded his head as he absorbed the information. "I hear what you're saying." He sent her a half-smile. "I know you did what you did for our people, but never," he pointed a finger at her as he stood, "do that again. Do you hear me, Hazel? You might be an adult, but I am your father and the leader of this colony. I can't have people running around doing whatever they want."

"Understood." Hazel stood. "Sorry." She mumbled, feeling like a kid once more.

He came around the table, wrapped his strong arms around her, and hugged her tight. "I'm just glad you're fine. When we found you missing, we weren't sure what to think."

"Please," she looked up at her father, "just promise me you will give him a fair chance to tell you what his people are thinking and don't hurt him." Her voice nearly cracked at the end of the sentence.

"You have my word that no harm will come to him." Her father promised before pulling away from the hug and motioning Theo away from the door. "People are going to want their lunch soon." He faced her as he pointed another finger at her. "No visiting the alien, Hazel. And I'll speak with you later."

"Thanks." Hazel sighed in relief as her father strode away and out of the cafeteria. She felt that the conversation had gone better than she could have hoped.

Theo remained, his steely grey eyes focused on her. "You have feelings for the alien."

It wasn't a question. It was a simple statement of truth.

Hazel didn't want to put Drakkein in Theo's bad graces, but she also didn't want to lie to anyone about what she felt. "I've gotten to know him." She agreed, not needing to go into the nitty gritty details. "I think if you allowed them a chance, the Aeci would grow on you as well."

Theo's eyes narrowed on her before he spun around and marched out of the cafeteria.

Ugh. He wasn't going to be her fan anymore. Then again, she didn't want his attention.

Pursing her lips, Hazel walked back to her room. If she wasn't allowed to see Drakkein then she should wash and change and come back for lunch to see if there was any information on Drakkein.

"Hazel!"

Glancing around, Hazel found the source of the voice. A hand waved in the air vigorously. She didn't even need to see the face to know who was waving at her. It was Maggie. As she came around a table full of people eating, Hazel spotted her friend.

"It's good to see you again!" Maggie said as Hazel placed her tray of food on the table.

"It's nice to be back and see everyone." Hazel agreed.

"When no one could find you, I worried you'd been stolen away by the aliens in the middle of the night." Maggie's eyes grew wide as she raised a dark-skinned hand to play with her black curly hair.

"Sorry," Hazel mumbled. "I knew people would be worried, but I also hoped you'd understand why I left without saying anything."

"I feel a bit hurt you couldn't trust me with your plans." Maggie shrugged. "But you didn't know how I'd react."

"How would you have reacted?"

"Called you nuts and begged you to rethink," Maggie admitted. "Although, I hope you know I wouldn't have ratted you out to your father or anyone else in the colony."

Hazel laughed, glad to be back with her friend. As she ate their bland rations, she found herself wishing she could be back in the Aeci city in their large food market. She would much rather be trying new and strange foods than be back here eating rations.

"I heard the aliens have large leathery wings, and that we have one here. What's he like?" Maggie asked as she ate her own plate of food.

"How did you miss the commotion?"

Maggie sighed over a forkful of ration. "I was tending to some of the animals when it all happened. By the time I got them put away, everything was over."

"Well, the alien's name is Drakkein, and he is amazing. Tall, strong, and drop-dead gorgeous." Hazel sighed as she remembered his face and body and those deep dark eyes that sucked her in. Even if they did find peace… or not, she couldn't imagine staying here in the human colony. She wanted to go back with Drakkein when he left, assuming he wanted her.

Maggie cocked her head to the side, her tight curly hair bobbing around her heart-shaped face. "From what I've heard, they are scary sounding. Large bodies with horns and leathery wings." She grimaced.

"They might look scary, but from I could tell, their people are decently friendly and just as curious about us as we are about them."

"I suppose I'll have to take your word for it." Maggie shrugged. "So, are we in talks for a peaceful resolution? Please, tell me we are. I don't think I can handle many more sleepless nights."

"I don't know," Hazel answered honestly. "It's in my father's hands now. I would say he wants peace as much as we do, though."

"Let's hope so. I don't like the idea of war, and I'm pretty sure no one else likes the idea any more than I do."

A scream of pain echoed through the cafeteria from outside.

"Did you hear that?" Hazel glanced around in alarm as she tried to figure out who could be screaming.

"It sounds like it came from the courtyard." Maggie rose from her seat, and Hazel followed her as Maggie led the way to the cafeteria doors.

When the doors to the cafeteria opened, Hazel's jaw dropped to the ground at what they revealed.

Drakkein kneeled on the sand of the yard. His hands were tied behind his back, and his wings bound, as well as his ankles. His silvery skin burned and blistered black as the rays of the sunlight touched his sensitive skin.

"What in the universe?" Maggie gasped in horror as she clasped her hands to her mouth. "What are you doing to this man?" She stepped forward as she pointed to the young men standing proudly beside Drakkein, including Theo.

More gasps echoed in Hazel's ears as people trickled out of the cafeteria and other parts of the compound.

Drakkein had been stripped of his armor, but thankfully his pants still covered some of his skin, helping to prevent sunburns.

"How could they do this?" Someone said from behind Hazel.

"Help me!" Hazel yelled as she finally regained her senses and lurched forward.

Maggie immediately fell in step with her as they launched themselves towards Drakkein. They both bent over him, shielding him from the sun with their bodies as they worked on the ties.

"Get away from him."

Hazel glanced up to see Theo striding towards her, and she knew he would wrestle her away from Drakkein. She braced herself for a fight while she continued to work on his ties.

Two people from the colony stepped into Theo's path and then more joined, forming a barrier between the men who would see Drakkein harmed. Then more people joined, a few coming to help her with the ties on Drakkein's hands and feet.

Once they had him untied, Hazel called out, "Help me get him to the shade."

With help, they carried him, using his arms

and legs to haul him over to the cooler shade.

"Drakkein?" Hazel bent down beside him. She wanted to touch him somewhere to reassure herself that he was still alive, but every part of him looked too charred to touch. "Oh, Drakkein."

His eyes cracked open, and he reached a charred hand up to cup one of her cheeks. "I might be burned, but did you see your people?"

She shook her head as she leaned her cheek into his hand.

"They came together to help me." He sent her a smile. "It's a good sign."

"It would have been even better had no one harmed you." Hazel countered.

"True." Drakkein closed his eyes. "But I won't die from these injuries. It will just take a bit of salve and healing, and I'll be back to my old self."

"What is going on over here?"

Hazel glanced up to see her father striding towards the hovering group of colonists.

"Who's responsible for this?" Her father bellowed as he caught sight of Drakkein lying on the ground.

"Theo and his friends." Hazel eagerly offered up the information.

"I saw them as well," Maggie said.

"And I"

"Me as well." A couple more voices joined in.

"What? Why?" Her father looked to her for the answer, but she simply shrugged.

She had a guess, but she didn't actually know why Theo had done what he had. She figured he was jealous of Drakkein and had taken his anger out on an easy target with the help of his friends.

"You'd have to ask Theo," Maggie said, her hands on her hips. "Can we get a doctor over here, or what?"

"Here I am." Doctor Rebecca strode over with a few male nurses and a stretcher. "Move out of the way." Rebecca waved her hands at Hazel like she was just some nosy animal to be shooed away.

"Is he going to be okay?" Hazel asked as she peered over the shoulders of the nurses.

"He just needs some burn cream and some pain killers. Then we can get him back to his people in case there's anything else that needs to be done." Rebecca said in a calm, even voice, giving Hazel confidence that everything really would be fine.

"I'm coming with you."

"That's fine," Rebecca said as she without even bothering to glance at Hazel.

The nurses rolled Drakkein onto the stretcher and lifted him before heading in the direction of their small clinic.

"Wait," her father snagged Hazel's shoulder with a hand. "I wanted to let you know the council has made their decision. We will seek peace with the aliens, and we will allow them a trial for the men who were involved, as well as Theo and his friends answering for what they did to Drakkein."

Her shoulders sagged as relief flew through her. "I'm glad to hear that." Hazel hugged her father. "Sorry, this colony didn't end up bringing us away from the complications of space and aliens."

Her father's chest vibrated with his laughter. "Even I was getting a bit bored with our day to day activities. A man can only clean out animal stalls and plant vegetables for so long before he longs for something else."

"I need to…" Hazel glanced to where the nurses disappeared around a corner.

"Go." Her father released her as he ushered her away. "See to your alien. We don't need him dying on us when we are already in hot water with the Aeci."

Hazel sped off in the direction of the hospital. He would be fine. Everything would be fine. She had to believe that.

Epilogue

Hazel rested her head on Drakkein's chest as they watched the Aeci city fly by on leathery wings while lying on his bed. She ran her hands over his silver-skinned chest, tracing the scars that now crisscrossed his skin.

"I'm glad you healed without too many scars." There were quite a few, but after burning most of his torso, arms, and a little bit of his back, it could have been worse. After their doctors tended to him, they'd sent him back with a message of peace.

Her father and the men on the council had met the aliens in the middle of the desert, where they'd hashed out the details for peace. It wouldn't be an overnight solution, but they were well on their way.

"I thought scars made a man sexy."

Hazel glanced up to see him wink at her. Her lips curved up in a smile. "It will only remind me of what happened to you. I still have nightmares about it." She shivered.

Drakkein used an arm to press her closer to his side. "We brought our people peace. Theo and his friends are in our jail for the murder and for torturing me."

That was one thing that had been resolved quickly. The trial was set, and after all the evidence from the scene, it was determined that Theo and his friends had acted out of anger rather than self-defense.

Hazel nodded her head. "Jail is where they should be. I worried during the whole trial that my people might not convict them. I should have held more faith in my people to do what is right."

Drakkein's hand roamed over her back. "If you miss them, we can go up and visit."

"Nah, my dad should be stopping by with some people to discuss some more things with your father and the Aeci council. I'll get a chance to speak with him then." She smiled at Drakkein. "I'm just grateful we could convince our people to let us live together."

"I haven't heard of this meeting." Drakkein's brows drew down over his eyes. "What is it about?"

Hazel frowned. "I don't know. I just heard something about my father coming down here. I guess we will find out tomorrow."

"In the meantime, I know how to pass the time." Drakkein flipped her onto her back, his wings spreading out above them, and Hazel giggled as he sucked one of her nipples into his mouth.

"Sounds good to me."

This story line will continue in another book with Maggie starring as a main character! Find the other Galactic Courtship books on Amazon! Thanks for reading.